A Treepoint Christmas

JAMIE BEGLEY

Young Ink Press Publication
YoungInkPress.com

Edited by CD Editing, Erin Toland,
& Diamond in the Rough Editing
Cover Art by CT Cover Creations

Connect with Jamie,
Facebook.com/AuthorJamieBegley
Instagram.com/authorjamiebegley
JamieBegley.net

Prologue

The snow began to fall when she hit Jamestown city limits, barely discernable droplets of water melting the instant they hit the windshield. Those that survived were swooshed away with one swish of the windshield wiper, as if the tiny dots never existed. Just like the small child she had carried, who had found life for a few tiny milliseconds on Earth.

As the bridge to Treepoint came into view, the snow started to blanket the ground. The flakes lasted a few seconds longer on the road than the ones on the window, the salt breaking it down to slush as the tires rolled over it until it was an ugly, muddy mess. Just as she had been broken and swept away by a trusted individual at fourteen. Manipulated, she had been thrust out of childhood and into the adult world she had no clue how to navigate, becoming putty in his hands.

Flipping the wipers onto high, she saw the bridge ahead. She didn't have to make the turn onto the bridge. She could keep driving on past, just keep going on. In three hours, she could be in Lexington. In four, Louisville. No one knew her in either cities. She could start over fresh. No one would know her name, that her parents had to sell their home because of how badly she had humiliated them, nor that she had nearly taken the life of a newborn, believing it to be hers when she hadn't been able to accept her own was dead.

To put the cherry on top of the mistakes she had made, the child she nearly killed was the President's of The Last Riders, a motorcycle club that had earned a reputation of being ruthless and never leaving a score unsettled.

So far, they had left her alone. She was sure her stay in a mental care facility for seventeen months had held their revenge in check.

Each day of the two years she had lived at a halfway house afterward, she expected it to be her last. Would they make her death look like an accident, or would they make it plain that The Last Riders had settled their score?

When she left the halfway house, there wasn't a night she didn't go to bed expecting to wake listening for any suspicious noises until exhaustion allowed her to sleep.

Working from home, she had lived a solitary existence until a week ago when she came to a stark conclusion—her life was so barren and miserable that death would be a blessing. Even God didn't care enough to put an end to her life, and she was too much of a coward to do it herself.

That was why she was going back to Treepoint. She had worked two remote jobs until she gave both jobs her notice. Packing up what little possessions she had, she filled her newly-purchased secondhand car with gas then started driving. She drove until she couldn't drive anymore then pulled over at a rest stop to sleep a few hours before driving again. She had one destination in mind—Treepoint.

When she switched her blinker on as she neared the bridge, the light turned red, preventing her from turning.

Staring at the red light, Megan knew it was an omen, warning her away from Treepoint.

When the light turned green, her foot remained on the brake, and a honking horn had a smile forming on her lips as she released the brake and made the turn onto the bridge.

She was surprised the old bridge didn't crumble beneath her as she crossed it; she had burned so many bridges before she was taken away. There wasn't one person in the whole town who would be happy she was back.

As she drove over the bridge, she thought of the person who had her cringing in humiliation at how terrible she had been. She couldn't blame anyone for not liking her; she didn't like herself.

She had paid her parents back what she'd owed them, volunteered countless hours to charities, but there were still amends that needed to be made.

She was going to spend one last Christmas in Treepoint, attempt to make amends to those she had wronged, and lay a headstone on a little child's grave, which remained unmarked.

The wheels of her car gave a bump as she came off the bridge, dragging her attention back to the present. She tightened her hands on the wheel as the snow grew heavier, the lines on the road barely visible. The road hadn't been salted here, and the snow on the road looked pretty and pristine, as if she was embarking on a journey into a winter wonderland.

Every mile she drove closer to Treepoint brought back the despair and helplessness of the life she had left behind. Going back wasn't going to change the past, but that wasn't why she was doing it, anyway. She was going back for two reasons.

She had to find out if she was mentally strong enough, that whatever the circumstances, she would be able to handle it this time without breaking and harming others. The scary part was if she failed and lost her sanity, which had been so hard to regain, for good. As scary as it was, she had to know. She wouldn't take a chance endangering anyone ever again.

Secondly, she wasn't going to live her life looking over her shoulder, waiting for The Last Riders to get their revenge. She was going to give them their shot. What they did with it was up to them. They couldn't hate her more than she hated herself.

Fifteen minutes later, she crossed over the small bridge which led to the main street. The small town hadn't aged well. Paint was peeling off some of the older businesses, the town's drug store was closed down, and weathered signs looked outdated and damaged.

As depressing as the sight of the town's further decline was, she also saw the cracked and broken sidewalks had been repaired and new business had been opened, which seemed encouraging, but the sight which truly showed the town was fighting to stay alive brought a sheen of tears to her eyes.

The same Christmas lights she would gaze wonderingly at when she was a little girl were attached to the streetlights, giving the town a festive atmosphere. Treepoint would never be described as a cheerful place to live, as many of the inhabitants were dirt poor and, despite their poverty, had no desire to leave their family or the mountains behind.

Treepoint was home. They had been born in the mountains. It was in their blood. The grass wasn't greener on the other side of the mountain, nor did the city lights beckon them away. With resignation, they lived the same life as their parents, and their parents had lived the same one their children would live. So many generations had grown up under their holiday glow ... as she had.

Swallowing down the lump in her throat, she fought back tears at the memories of the Christmases she had experienced here. It was a special time of the year, when everyone was welcomed to join in the festivities regardless of how well liked they were.

If the people of Treepoint were ever going to allow her back within their midst, it would be during Christmas.

Christmas was meant to be a celebration of life, to share love, hope, and faith with family and friends, not crying in a lonely apartment, watching the lights on a Christmas tree blinking alone.

She didn't expect to find absolution for her sins just because it was Christmas. What she was desperately searching for was to make peace before she said a final goodbye to Treepoint, embarking on a new future somewhere else ... if The Last Riders let her have one.

One

Continuing through town, she stayed on the two-lane road as it began to climb a mountain. Her fear ratcheted higher as she neared her destination. Then, with sweaty palms, she turned the steering wheel into The Last Riders' parking lot.

She thought she would throw up when a group of bikers standing by their bikes broke off their conversation to stare at her as she got out of the car. Clenching her teeth together so hard her jaw hurt, she walked confidently toward the factory and opened the door.

Male and female eyes swung toward the door as it closed behind her. The workplace chatter came to an abrupt stop, their friendly gazes turning chilled as they recognized her.

One man, who had been loading packages onto a cart, dropped the package with a loud *thump* before striding toward her. Recognizing The Last Rider as Train, she braced herself to be thrown out.

"What do you want?"

She wanted to run at the aggressive tone and barely

managed to contain her composure. "I'd like to speak to Loker James, if he's available."

His eyes pierced, boring into hers. "Do you have an appointment?"

"No."

"Then make one," he snapped, taking a step forward and opening the door.

She remained where she was, but turned around to face him, "We both know he won't answer my call if I did." Standing resolute, she had to lock her knees to keep her legs from shaking.

Train let the door close, raking her face with a stern gaze. "Stay here. I'll see if he's available."

Nodding, she waited as he took out a cell phone and began texting.

As she watched Train, she heard a sound to the side. Turning her head, she heard a door open. Her heart skipped a beat at seeing the man standing in the doorway.

Shade.

They silently stared at each other until she was the one who broke the tense silence.

"Shade." Proud her voice didn't come out in a squeak, she steeled herself once more to be thrown out.

"Megan." Shade's expression, nor his tone, gave any indication at how he felt seeing her. His eyes then moved to Train.

"She wants to talk with Viper. I just texted him," Train explained.

"You can wait in the office."

Burying her hands in her coat, she walked to the office door and went inside, then moved toward the desk, but didn't take one of the two chairs positioned in front. She clenched her hands in fear when she heard the door close, only to relax when she found the room was empty.

Would it be bad manners to sit? she asked herself.

Afraid her legs would give out because they were trembling so badly, she sat down, keeping to the edge so she could stand up quickly if she had to.

She had just managed to get her nerves under control when she heard the door open. Turning her head, she was glad the chair was under her. Too frightened to move, she remained seated.

"Thank you for seeing me, Mr. James." She focused on her words, keeping the quiver of fear out of her voice as Loker James moved further into the office with Shade following. Viper went to sit behind the desk while Shade closed the door then took the chair next to her.

"You wanted to talk to me?"

Bowing her head, she kept her eyes focused on the denim covering her knees. Unlike Shade, Viper made it plain what he thought of her—a mixture of antagonism and dislike was easily discernible on his harsh features.

"Yes, I appreciate you taking the time to talk with me. I didn't think you would agree to see me if I called."

"I wouldn't have," he replied coldly. "But since you're here, go ahead."

Megan opened her mouth to begin the prepared speech she had written over a thousand times over the years and had memorized so she wouldn't make a fool of herself in front him.

Under her downcast lashes, she saw Viper lift a hand to stop her.

"If you're here to apologize for nearly killing my daughter when she was in the NICU, let me save you some air. I'm never going to accept the apology bec—"

"I know you won't," she interrupted him. "I wouldn't, either. Neither you, nor Winter, can hate me more than I hate myself. There isn't a day that has gone by that I don't wish it hadn't happened. Your wife was the kindest person to me in town. She was more upset when I quit school than my parents were."

Megan was unaware her voice had grown hoarser the longer she talked.

"Mrs. James always made me feel smarter than I was. My mother used to tell me I wasn't the brightest shade at the makeup counter, and she was right," she said self-depreciatively. "I was terrible in school. I just never seemed able to focus enough to study to make good grades. I couldn't finish a book because I read at a snail's pace, then I'd get frustrated at how stupid I was when I fell further and further behind. Mrs. James did everything to try to help me. She offered to tutor me and gave me extra time to make up assignments I couldn't complete on time. I didn't take any of the help she offered and married Curt." She felt the taste of bile in her mouth after she spoke her late husband's name.

"That, in itself, shows how stupid I was."

Viper and Shade sat silently as she talked, listening.

"Winter was everything I wanted to be and never could be. I was jealous of how smart she is, the respect everyone gave her. I was even jealous of how you treated her. I saw you help her into a truck as if she was the most precious thing in your world. The way you looked at her is how I knew you would never accept any apology from me."

She was relieved she had kept her head downcast. She didn't want them to see the tears she was holding back.

"When they told me my child"—her voice cracked, but she continued, hoping they hadn't noticed—"was gone, I didn't want to believe it ... that I was never going to be able to hold her. I wanted to hold my baby before they took her, but Curt insisted they get *it* out of the room. Then he went off on me about being a failure, that I couldn't do anything right, that if I was too stupid to hold down a job, how did I think I was going to be a good mother? He told me he wanted a divorce, that I was a failure as a wife and a mother."

Curt had said more cruel things to her, which Megan didn't repeat to the men.

"After he left, I don't know what happened. I just kind of zoned out. I lost my child and my husband on the same day. I couldn't lose both of them. I went to go after Curt, and I walked into the nursery. I don't know why I thought my baby would be in there ... Then I saw the incubator ... and the baby inside ... The last name ... it was Mrs. James' and your child. I was so jealous ... She had it all—a job, a husband, and a child."

Feeling the warm wetness on her hands, she unclenched them in her pockets.

"I don't know how it got twisted in my head that Mrs. James' baby was mine ... Everyone was there for her. I had no one. When my nurse called my parents to tell them I was in the hospital, they hung up on her ... I could have died, and neither Curt nor my parents would have cared enough to claim my body." Megan bit down on her bottom lip to keep it from trembling.

"I'm sickened at myself for my behavior. There isn't a day that goes by when I don't see you trying to get in the door ... or see myself taking your baby out of the incubator ..." Clearing her throat, Megan forced herself to go on.

"Like I said, I don't expect forgiveness from either you or your wife. I came here because both of you deserve to hear I'm moving back to Treepoint. I'm going to stay at the hotel until I can find an apartment. I didn't want to suddenly show up and her seeing me without warning. I called the school to make sure she was there before coming here. I'll make sure I'll stay out of both your ways. You also have no need to fear. I will never go near your daughter. I completely understand if your hatred of me makes it untenable that I live here in Treepoint."

She pulled her hand out of her pocket, holding a slip of paper, and laid it on the desk in front of Viper. "Curt had a life insurance policy, but I don't want a dime of it. I want you to put it in a trust for your daughter. If you don't want her to have it, give it to charity or rip up the cheque. It's your decision." Megan rose from the chair to meet Viper's gaze directly for the first time. "When I find a place to rent, I'll call Shade here at the factory to give him the address and what job I find."

She steadily walked toward the door and reached for the doorknob.

"I'm aware I treated everyone in this town abysmally, and I'm truly embarrassed. But could you do me a favor and tell Mrs. James I got my GED? She is a good person, and she may hate me, but when I dropped out, she was worried I wouldn't. Tell her I did it for her. School was a nightmare for me. I only finished because I knew Mrs. James took it as a personal failure that I quit. I can't rewind how I acted when I lost my child, but that, I could fix. Mrs. James never failed me. I failed myself."

Two

Neither Viper nor Shade attempted to stop her.

Megan maintained her poise until she was back inside her car. Tears were already sliding down her cheeks as she pulled onto the road leading away from The Last Riders' compound. Blinking her eyes so she could see the road, she noticed a vehicle sitting off to the side. She thought someone had broken down and had left, but a flash of movement caught her eye.

She slowed the car on the slope of the mountain and saw a man staring up at a tree. Looking in the direction he was, Megan found a huge orange cat clutching the tree trunk. She pulled off the road behind the SUV and got out.

As she made her way over the frozen ground, the man turned his head.

Goooolllyyy jeez. Megan had seen men as gorgeous as him in magazine, but had never encountered one out in the wild before.

"Hey." His friendly grin was the first one she had received since entering Treepoint.

Megan couldn't help but to respond, despite her unease at

being in such an isolated spot. "Hey. Looks like your friend is in a predicament."

The man's hands went to his hips in frustration as his head tilted back to look at the cat. "Never met him in my life. I would have left him there if I wasn't responsible for him being there."

Grabbing a huge tuft of grass to heave herself up the slope to stand next to him, she asked, "What did you do? Bark at him?"

His appreciative laugh filled her with a warmth she hadn't felt in a long time, if ever.

"Not exactly. He was sitting in the middle of the road. I was afraid he was going to get hit, so I pulled off. When I went to pick him up, he took off and climbed the tree."

Megan lifted her chin, gauging the distance from the ground to the limb the cat was sitting on. "Wow. He's pretty far up."

"Yes, he is, and he doesn't seem to have any intention of coming down anytime soon."

"No, he doesn't," she agreed as the cat started to delicately lick its paw. "Any idea how you're going to get him down?"

His eyes twinkled with laughter. "I go back and forth between climbing the tree or leaving his ass."

Her lips twitched in laughter. "What side is winning?"

"Put it this way: if you hadn't pulled off, I would have already been gone. Something about that cat makes me believe he's not going to appreciate any effort I make."

The cat lifted its paw to study it then continued to lick.

"I'm getting that impression, too."

The man quirked an eyebrow at her. "Do you have any ideas? I'm open to suggestions."

"I vote you climb the tree," she suggested.

He gave her a strange look before shaking his head. "I'm afraid of heights."

"Oh." Megan gauged the distance again. "I guess I could try. The tree has a few knots. I climbed a few trees when I was younger."

"Only if you want to give it a go. I can give you lift, if that helps."

Nodding, she braced her hand on the tree as he cupped his hands for her to step on.

"Ready?" he asked.

"I think so."

Placing her foot into his cupped hands, she found herself lifted upward. Grabbing at the tree trunk, she managed to grab two thick knots. She looked upward. She was just two limbs from the cat, who was staring at her balefully.

What in the hell was she doing? She hated cats. Hated them from the time she was a little girl and a neighbor's cat would crap in her sandbox.

Digging the side of her shoes into the tree trunk, she managed to climb to the limb below the cat.

"Be careful." the man called out. "By the way, what's your name?"

"Megan."

"Mine's Cole. It's nice to meet you."

Jesus Christ, does his voice have to match his looks? she complained to herself as she pulled herself higher.

"Here, kitty, kitty ..." she crooned softly. When she reached the limb the cat was on, she gingerly extended her arm, expecting the cat to jump at any second.

The cat stretched on the limb before standing. Then, like a ballet dancer on a high wire, it walked toward her. Megan couldn't believe it when the cat rubbed against her hand.

Carefully lifting the cat off the limb and into her arm, she held it to her chest. He rubbed his head under her chin, and a soft purr emitted from the feline, sending vibrations to her chest.

"Aw … He's so sweet. He's letting me hold him."

Megan thought Cole said something under his breath, but she couldn't make it out.

"What did you say?"

"How are you going to hold on to him coming down?"

"You couldn't have asked that question before I climbed the tree?"

"I didn't think of it. To be honest, I didn't think you would be able to get him. I thought he would jump."

Megan looked down to find him staring up at her. "I did, too." She laughed. "I'm going to try to edge down."

Slowly, she scooted one foot down, then her other one. Using the back of the forearm while holding the cat, she managed to snuggle the cat more to the middle of her chest, freeing her hand. Nervous, she waited to be scratched at any moment, but she was surprised when the cat remained still as she slid down the tree.

"I've got you." Warm hands gripped her around the waist, lifting her off the tree.

"Should I put her down?"

Cole gave a wry grimace. "Not unless you want to climb the tree again."

"I'll pass. Here you go." She peeled the cat off her chest and held it out for him to take.

Shaking his head at her, he took a step back and nearly slid down the slope. "What am I supposed to do with it?"

"I don't know, but I can't keep him. I'm staying at the hotel."

"You don't live here?"

"Not until I find an apartment."

"I'm only visiting. I can't take a cat back to where I'm staying."

"You don't live here?"

"No, I'm only visiting until Christmas. Is there an animal shelter close by?"

"Yes, about three miles. Here." Without giving him a choice, Megan thrust the cat into his arms. "There you go. Problem solved. It closes at five, or it used to. You should be going, or you're going to be stuck with him for the night."

Ignoring the cat's beseeching eyes, she felt guilty. What did she know about taking care of cats? Hell, she barely managed to take care of herself. The cat was better off at a shelter than if she were responsible for it.

"You need me to write out the directions for the shelter?" Jumping the rest of way down the slope, she found her footing, turning to find him following more cautiously.

"No, thanks. My car has GPS."

They walked next to each other to his car, where he paused before getting inside. "Thanks for your help."

"You're welcome."

"I'll be here until after Christmas. Would you want to go out for coffee while I'm in town?"

"I'm sure I'll see you in town. Bye, Cole."

Once upon a time, she would have jumped at a chance to have coffee with a man like Cole. Stupid shit would have come out of her mouth in a spat of word vomit, showing how stupid she was taking Cole up on the invitation so quickly that the stunning man would get whiplash. Half of the reason she was in Treepoint was to prove to herself that she was capable of making the right decisions. Going out with Cole, even for a friendly cup of coffee, wouldn't be a smart decision. He was only going to be in town for a short time, and she had no clue how long she would decide to stay, or even if she had a future at all if The Last Riders came after her for retribution.

Restraint had never been her strong suit, but she was going to ignore the *omg-he's-so-freaking-cute* her old self was screaming inside her head and get her ass back in the car before she changed her mind.

"I guess I'll see you around, then. Goodbye, Megan."

The disappointment in his eyes almost made her reconsider. With reluctant footsteps, she returned to her car.

Cole's hand motioned out of his car window for her to go first.

"Dammit! He's a gentleman, too." Giving him a small wave as she drove past his vehicle, Megan knew she had made the best decision not only for herself but for Cole. She was actually doing him a favor.

How often had Curt told her she was worse than Typhoid Mary? He had been right ... he had the proof ... Curt was as dead as a doornail.

Now that she was away from Cole, her shoulders straightened. She had made the right decision. That dude was too magnificent to find himself in an early grave.

Three

＄elf-consciously, Megan drove, intermittently glancing in her rearview mirror at the vehicle driving behind. Flipping on her blinker, she made the turn into the hotel lot, unable to resist a final glance at the white SUV before finding an empty spot in front of the office. As she got out of the car, a growling sound came from her stomach. Her appetite had been non-existent as she had traveled to Treepoint. Yet, judging by the prolonged grumbling sounds, it seemed it was back.

Her hunger evaporated again, though, when she saw who was behind the counter, talking on her cell phone.

Pretending not to recognize the woman she had gone to high school with, Megan stepped up to the counter. "I have a room reserved."

Putting the cell phone down, the hotel clerk gave her a critical stare. Megan felt more judged than when she had been discussed by a panel of mental health experts for her evaluation.

"Name?"

"Megan Smith."

Chelsea's lips pursed in disapproval. "Don't you mean Megan Dawkins?"

Megan didn't flinch at the insulting way her former classmate spoke to her.

"The reservation is under Megan Smith," she said without infliction. Megan would be damned if she was going to give Chelsea something to gossip about other than she was back in town.

Chelsea made no attempt to key the information into the computer, and Megan was treated to her expression turning even more pinched. "I thought you were still in prison."

"I was never in prison," Megan corrected the mistaken belief she was sure had been swirled around the town gossip mill.

"Oh, that's right." Chelsea stared at her belittlingly. "They sent you off to the loony bin, didn't they?"

Megan met her gaze directly without shying away. "I spent several months in a mental care hospital."

Chelsea's lashes lowered to half-mast. "Call it whatever you want." Disparagingly, she clicked her tongue as she began typing on the computer.

Her expression became grimmer when Chelsea must have seen she had paid for her stay in full. She opened the drawer and took out an envelope and a plastic card before inserting the card inside of a tiny machine attached to her computer. After pulling the card out, she slipped it into the envelope to hand it to her.

Megan reached for the card but raised her eyes when Chelsea didn't release it from her grip.

"You're in 312. I hope you're not planning on freaking out in your hotel room. You'll be responsible for any damage I find. If I hear any commotion," she warned, "I'm calling the sheriff so fast your head will spin."

Taking the card when Chelsea finally released it, she leaned against the counter, as if settling in for a long chat. "You know, I didn't like you in high school."

Chelsea made a face, which seemed to say she was in complete agreement.

"We don't have to be friends now, either."

"You wish," Chelsea snapped sarcastically.

"No, actually, I don't. I saw how you treated your best friends. You bullied them until they had to get your permission on what color they wore each day, or what they brought to eat for lunch. I bet, after you graduated, not a one of them gave you the time of day anymore."

Chelsea's face turned ugly. "Then you'd be wrong. We still talk."

"Maybe so, but you're the one calling them, not the other way around."

Straightening from the counter, Megan walked away, not caring about the hatred Chelsea made no effort to hide.

Before getting back in her car, she checked the room number of the door closest to where she was standing. Gauging where her room should be from where she was, Megan got back in her car and circled the parking lot, studying the numbers and eventually finding hers. The parking lot only had two other cars in it.

Chelsea had given her the room directly behind the office. Wryly twisting her lips as she wheeled her suitcase toward the room, Megan gave it one day before Chelsea called the sheriff on her.

In high school, she had earned a reputation for going after anyone who looked at her the wrong way, much less said something she didn't like. Megan had gotten on her bad side a couple of times and had paid the price each time.

She locked the door behind her and heaved the suitcase onto the bed. The sound of the headboard hitting the wall made her wince. There went getting something to eat. Instead of unpacking, she sat down on the bed to wait. It didn't take long.

Megan saw the blue lights through the curtains. Standing, she went to open the door before she heard the knock.

She recognized the police officer getting out of his patrol car, and she didn't miss the surprise on his face that she had beat him to the door.

"Hello, Knox, come on in."

Four

Megan heard the bell ring over her head as she walked inside the diner. The diner had been a popular place to hang out or grab a quick meal when she lived there. Waitresses came and went regularly, which was why she was there. During the last week, she had applied for several jobs, with no success. Waitressing was the last thing she wanted to do, considering her track record, but she was running out of options.

The restaurant was completely empty for the time being. Megan didn't think she could ever remember the diner being completely empty.

As she came inside, a heavyset man appeared from the back of the restaurant. His hostile expression made her want to turn tail and run. Why had no one ever told her desperation gave you courage?

Walking forward under his scrutiny, she took the first old-fashioned pivoting seat at the counter.

The man lumbered across to where she was sitting to slam a menu down in front of her. Megan didn't look at the menu, afraid it would set off her rumbling stomach again.

"Hello."

"What do you want?"

Taken aback at how rude he was being, her mind drew a blank as to what to say.

"I don't have all damn day."

Mentally shaking herself, she forced a pleasant smile. "I'd like to apply for a job."

His beady eyes went half-mast. "Look around you; does it look like I need any fucking help?"

Megan didn't bother to look around; she had seen how empty the restaurant was when she entered. And she was too hungry to take no for an answer immediately, especially since she didn't recognize him.

"I can do anyth—"

The sound of the bell over the door had her head turning to watch Dustin Porter coming inside.

She watched as he walked skittishly toward the counter, her jaw dropping upon seeing the tentative way Dustin was behaving.

"What do you want?"

Feeling better that Dustin was treated to the same rudeness, Megan watched in wonder as one of the Porter brothers seemed leery of someone. Usually, it was the other way around. The Porters were known to be loose cannons when you made one of them angry.

"I'll take five deluxe bags."

Taking a pad and ink pen out of his dirty apron, the rude man scrawled the order onto the pad before tearing the thin strip of paper off. He slapped the thin paper onto the counter before the beady-eyed man watched Dustin pick up the paper like a snake getting ready to strike.

"Ten minutes."

"I'll wait outside," Dustin replied, already walking backward.

"Do that."

Megan caught the triumphant smile on the man's face as Dustin pivoted on his heels and practically ran out of the restaurant.

"You going to order something or waste more of my time?"

"I was asking about a job," Megan reminded him.

"Don't need anyone. I prefer working by myself."

"I'll take part-time."

He lumbered off while she was still talking to him.

Damn him, she needed the job. There were only three places left where she could apply, and none of them were viable options.

"I'll work part-time." Megan raised her voice, uncaring if she was making a fool of herself. "I'll work for tips, for food ... Please, I'm desperate."

She didn't bother to turn around at the sound of the bell, assuming Dustin had come back for his order.

"I was beginning to doubt if I was going to see you again."

At the familiar voice coming from behind her, she started to turn as Cole took the seat next to her.

"Hey," she greeted him, the despondent feeling lifting at the warm way he was looking at her. Somehow, Cole made her feel as if they had been friends for years.

She hadn't had a friend since grade school, someone to tell all of her secrets to, nor hang out with or make plans to go somewhere. Anytime someone had made the effort, she had brushed their attempts away. She had been strong to walk away when Cole asked her out for coffee, but Megan didn't think she was strong enough to do the same today.

The door swinging open from the kitchen had Megan bracing herself to be thrown out.

"What you want?"

Unlike Dustin, Cole greeted Marty with a friendly grin. "Hey, Marty, how are you doing?"

"How in the fuck do you think I'm doing?" he snarled. "I'm fucking working here, aren't I?"

Cole didn't take offense, his grin staying in place. Then, rubbing his hands together as if he were cold, Cole gave his order. "I'll take a number seven premium bag with a Coke." Curious, Cole looked at her. "What are you having?"

"I'm not …" She was about to tell Cole she wasn't hungry, but Marty interrupted her.

"She's taking her pretty time ordering."

"Ah … it's a hard choice, isn't it?"

She was so hungry that she had planned to take some ketchup and mustard packets from the condiment buckets sitting on the counter before she left.

"Kind of."

Meeting Marty's eyes, she didn't finish what she had originally been about to say.

"Let me help. I have Marty's menu memorized. I also owe you for helping me get that cat out of the tree, so your lunch will be my treat."

As hungry as she was, Megan couldn't accept his offer. She wanted to prove she could stand on her on two feet without breaking. Before she could refuse, though, Cole sidetracked her.

"Have you eaten here before?"

"I've eaten here before, but not since he's"—Meg nodded her head at the man behind the counter—"taken over."

"Marty, give Megan the grand bag." Cole tilted his head to the side to whisper, "You can thank me later. You need the biggest bag because everyone who tastes his burgers for the first time always wants more. What you don't eat, you can take for leftovers, but I bet you'll finish the whole bag."

By the time Cole finished talking, Marty had scrawled the order down and slammed the paper down on the counter.

"Fifteen minutes."

"Cool." Unaffected by Marty's glower, Cole pivoted his chair toward her. "You want to join me at one of the booths?" Conspiratorially whispering, he added, "Typically, Marty prefers the customers to wait outside. Maybe he'll forget we're here if we hide in the corner booth."

Consoling herself that it would be rude to leave the restaurant after he had ordered food for her, Megan slid off the chair. "I'd like that. How does he stay in business if he doesn't want customers to eat inside?"

"Wait until you eat his burgers. Marty is half the reason I come to visit Treepoint."

"What's the other half?" Megan prepared herself not to show any reaction if Cole told her his girlfriend lived in Treepoint.

"My friends come to visit The Last Riders."

Five

As she followed Cole to the booth, her heart sank with each step. Standing, Cole waited until she sat before sliding into the booth on the opposite side.

Come on, Megan; it's not like you had a chance with him, anyway, she berated herself. Men like Cole could have any woman they wanted. Girls like her never got the happily ever afters, because they didn't deserve their dreams coming true. Curt had taught her that she needed to put herself first, and to hell with the rest. She had put herself first and had hurt a lot of people along the way. What Curt hadn't told her was: she would lose a piece of herself with hurt she inflicted until the only part of her true self remaining was an empty shell with no family, friends, or acquaintances giving her a shot glass of water if she was dying of thirst.

Pretending an interest in the traffic driving past the restaurant, Megan didn't make a remark about his friendship with The Last Riders. If he mentioned her name to them, her whole life's history would be an open book.

Megan felt an overwhelming sadness that her past mistakes would prevent her from getting to know Cole better.

"I'm glad I ran into you today."

The kindness in his eyes made her want to confess her past mistakes before someone else could.

Blinking back the tears stinging her eyes, Megan turned away from the window. "Did you have any trouble finding the animal shelter?"

"None." His handsome features cracked into a relieved smile. "I checked in on him today and found out Rascal has been adopted by a little girl. I have to admit it lifted a huge weight off my chest," Cole confessed. "I felt terrible I couldn't adopt him himself."

"Do you like cats?" Megan forced herself to talk normally as she continued the conversation. Chalking it up to yet another reason to regret the mistakes of her youth, she was tempted to make up a hasty excuse and leave. But that was the easy way out, and she didn't have to face any ramifications of her actions if she ran. No, she deserved to have to sit here, knowing when this sweet man found out she had nearly killed a child, he would never talk to her again.

"Not necessarily. I'm more of a dog person. I don't have any pets, but my sister and her husband have a whole menagerie."

"What animals do they have?" she asked thickly.

Megan missed the searching look Cole gave her when she heard the bell ring. Dustin began walking to the cash register, then spotted them sitting in the booth and changed directions.

"Hey, Cole," he said, shooting an anxious glance to the front of the restaurant before turning back to Cole. "Wish I knew you were coming here. I would have asked you to pick up our orders."

"Sorry." Cole's face filled with amusement. "Next time, I'll send out a mass text."

"Do that. I'll give you gas money. Shit, I'd drive you here myself rather than face that son of a—"

"Come and get this fucking order. I have other orders on the grill."

Dustin rushed toward the counter, bumping into a chair and sending it askew. "Sorry." He reached for his wallet and handed Marty several bills.

After putting all the bills in the register, Marty slammed the cash drawer closed then turned to head back into the kitchen.

"What about my change?"

Marty gave Dustin the same beady-eyed stare he had given her. "You didn't want me to keep the change?"

Slowly, Dustin reached out for the bags of food he had ordered, holding them protectively against his chest. Then he took a step away from the register. "Keep the change."

"That's what I thought. Stop wasting my fucking time!"

He waited until Marty had disappeared back into the kitchen before moving an inch, and Megan could practically see the steam coming from Dustin's ears when he returned to where they were sitting.

"See you later, Cole."

Her heart started pumping wildly when his gaze switched to hers.

"Heard you were back in town."

"Last week." She nodded.

"Treepoint hasn't changed much since you left." Dustin's eyes pierced hers.

"I didn't expect it to." Megan didn't shy away from his gaze.

Dustin gave her a wry smile. "Hang in there. It gets better."

Megan gave a trembling one in return. "I'll keep that in mind."

Juggling his bags, he gave her a small lift of his chin. "Take care."

"Thanks, I will."

Cole stared at her curiously after Dustin left. "What was that about?"

"I—"

Both she and Cole jumped when their food was slammed down onto the table.

"You can get your own damn drinks."

"Will do. Thanks, Marty."

She wrapped her hand around the full sugar dispenser, ready to brain him if he went for Cole.

"You're welcome."

Cole opened the two bags and started taking the food out, missing Marty's smirk when he saw the protective way she was gripping the sugar.

"Do you need some ketchup?" Cole asked innocently, unaware of the exchange.

"Please." She took the ketchup from Cole without taking her eyes off Marty until he was out of sight.

"He grows on you." Cole laughed, dipping a fry into the ketchup.

Megan shuddered. "God, I hope not."

"I'm going to grab our drinks." Laughing, Cole rose to his feet. "What can I get you?"

"Surprise me."

Picking up the small hamburger, which was similar in size to a White Castle, she took a bite. Sure she was mistaken, she took another bite.

"Darn."

Cole set two colas down on the table. "Better than you anticipated?"

"I refuse to answer on the grounds it may incriminate me."

"You don't have to. Marty makes the best burgers in twelve states."

Megan swallowed the last bite of her burger and reached for another. "On which list?"

"Mine, so I can attest to its accuracy."

Megan had to cover her mouth, unable to keep from laughing.

As they ate, the bell rang numerous times. In each instance, they would place an order then go outside to wait.

"It's definitely the food that is keeping him in business."

"For now." Cole grew more serious. "Eventually, they'll get tired of having to stand out in the cold just to get a hamburger, regardless how good it is. Spring is a long time away."

An idea came to her as Cole talked. She placed her hand over his. "Do you happen to know if there are any delivery drivers in Treepoint?"

Cole shrugged, giving her hand covering his a strange look. "I have no idea. Why?"

"Because ..." Megan laughed. "People in town might dislike me, but they may hate him."

Six

"Why do people dislike you?"

Megan had no one to blame but herself. She had lowered her guard in the excitement at potentially being able to get out of the financial straits which were becoming more dire each day.

"Am I the only one who wants to chow down?"

Her plan to out herself had come and gone. She liked the way he made her feel special.

Cole studied her as he placed the burger he was about to eat down. "Why do you think people dislike you?"

Megan pushed her food away. He wasn't going to be sidetracked.

Cole pushed it back. "Eat," he ordered. "You look like a hard wind would blow you away. We can talk when you're finished."

Megan ate halfheartedly, all the enjoyment from the food gone.

"Megan," he said gently.

She lifted a tear-filled gaze. The lump in her throat disappeared at the compassionate look he gave her.

"It's going to be okay. I'm a pretty chill guy. Nothing you could tell me is going to shock me or make me think of you any differently than when I came into the restaurant."

"You say that now, but you will," she replied numbly, forcing herself to take another bite.

"Maybe you'll feel more comfortable if I told you about myself. I'm originally from Queen City. Currently, I live in Marina del Rey when I'm not visiting my sister, Casey, and her family. I also take motorcycle trips with friends of Casey's husband, Max. They visit The Last Riders, and I visit a man who I owe everything I am, and everything I will be."

Becoming enthralled in what Cole was telling her about his life, she forgot about unintentionally revealing the town's dislike of her. Her appetite returned, and she ate without focusing on the internal recriminations which had been swarming through her mind like an angry beehive.

"Who was that?"

"Greer Porter."

Megan eyed Cole doubtfully. "Dustin's brother?"

"Yes." Cole's lips turned up at the corners. "You know Greer?"

"Everyone in town knows Greer. He's kind of hard to miss." As she said that, a sudden thought came to mind. "Although, now that you've mentioned him, I haven't seen him since I've been in town."

"Greer doesn't get out much anymore. He had a stroke."

Megan placed a hand over her mouth, stunned at the news. "Is he okay?" she asked in concern.

"He isn't back to his old self yet. His wife and brothers say he's good, but you can tell he's missing the spark that everyone says drives them crazy."

Megan set her hand back on the table. "But not you?"

"No, not me. I've seen the real Greer."

They stared at each other, cognizant Greer was more than the good ol' boy he pretended to be.

"I've seen the real Greer, too."

Cole put his elbows on the table to lean forward. "How?"

Megan shook her head. "You first."

Cole nodded. "That's fair." He straightened, running a hand through his blond hair. "This is hard to start. I really don't like talking about this ..."

"Then we don't have to—"

"No, I want to. I was going to tell you, anyway. I can't ask you to share your life with me if I'm not willing to share mine."

"Most men do," she said wryly.

"I'm not like most men."

Megan nearly rolled her eyes at that one. No, he wasn't. Cole was so handsome she had found her faith in God again. Only He could have created someone so stunningly beautiful.

Treepoint had more than its fair share of good-looking men, but there was a difference with Cole. He had such a gentle glow about him, as if the beauty on his face mirrored the heart within. His muscular frame made her feel protected, not afraid, as Curt's had. He didn't make small digs at her, thinking she was too stupid to understand he was making fun of her, nor did he say ugly remarks behind people's back. So far, she could only find one fault with him.

Cole was making her fall in love with him.

Seven

Megan managed to find her voice despite coming to the conclusion she was staring at the face of her next heartbreak. "I would agree with that."

"I hope you mean that in a good way." His good humor turned thoughtful. "I'm trying to think of a polite way to describe Casey and my mother." Giving a defeated sigh, Cole gave her a wry smile. "Put it this way: the only person our mother cares about is herself. She doesn't have a maternal bone in her body. When we grew up, she would get involved with men who ... let's just say weren't father material, either. She had the uncanny ability to lure men into spending money until they would bankrupt themselves. Those were the ones she used, keeping Casey and me hidden away from them. The men she married were in a different category. They were useless pieces of shit, making her give them the money she had talked the other men out of.

"As soon as I was old enough, I took off. I knew if I didn't get out of there, one or both of us would be dead. I wanted to take Casey with me, but my mother wouldn't let me. I didn't have a job or a place to stay, so getting custody of her was impossible. I found a job in construction, worked my ass off twenty hours a day, determined to get custody of my sister When I finally had enough to afford an apartment where I could give Casey her own bedroom, I just needed enough money saved to hire a lawyer to help me get custody.

"The day I earned enough money to pay a retainer fee, I received a call. My father had died, and Casey and I were the beneficiaries of his insurance policy. I went to get Casey. Her suitcases were packed, and my mother was doing what she could to convince Casey to stay, telling her that she would force me to spend all my money on legal fees if she went with me. I had to leave her that day. My lawyer finally helped me get custody of my sister when I showed pictures of my mother being abused by her husband.

"The day I was awarded custody, I drove to get her. My mother had been too nice to me when I told her I was on my way—that should have been my first clue."

Megan's hand tightened over Cole's, sensing what he had gone through was horrific from the way he was talking.

"I should have told Casey to meet me downstairs, or Mom bring her to the police station. But I didn't. I thought I could handle Mason. What I didn't count on was him bashing my head in with a steel pipe when Casey went to get her suitcases."

She couldn't prevent her shocked gasp, sickened at what Casey and Cole had to deal with, with no help from their mother.

"Casey managed to call 911 before Mason started beating her with the pipe. There isn't a doubt in my mind that both of us would have been dead by the time the police arrived. Casey told me I was barely clinging to life for months, in a coma. During that time, my mother managed to get Casey to lie to get the charges dropped on Mason by saying we were the ones who attacked him. She also tried to have my life support turned off and managed to convince Casey to hand over her inheritance so she could protect me.

"When I came out of the coma, I had the mental capacity of a five-year-old. I think Casey was being generous when she told me that. I can't tell you how, but if not for Greer, I still would be."

"You don't have to say how." There were those who were meant to be angels walking on Earth to share their beauty, then there were the chosen few who were placed on Earth meant to be at the right place, at the right time, to protect angels in distress ...

Self-loathing kicked in at remembering the child Greer had saved because of the actions she had caused.

Not wanting Cole to see her cry, she looked out the window. Guilt ate at her. She had tried to change everything about herself, to accept every punishment given to her. She had tried to make amends the best way she could. It still wasn't enough. It never would. She would live with the guilt for the rest of her life.

How could Cole's mother not have protected her children, then went so far as to steal from them? The longer she thought about it, the angrier she became.

"It's okay, Megan. You can look at me. I'm used to people feeling weird about me when they find out I had damage—"

Her head whipped back to him. "Weird isn't how I feel. I'm so darn angry I could spit."

"You don't look angry." Cole reached out to gently brush her tears away. "You're crying."

"I cry when I'm angry." She sniffled. "Your mother better hope she never meets me. I'll ... I'll ..." Megan broke off, falling under the spell of his angelic smile. "I'll pray for her."

Cole laughed. "That wasn't what you were about to say."

Wanting to fan herself at the tide of heat she could feel

coloring her cheeks, she hastily picked up her soda to hide her embarrassment behind the glass.

"I've forgiven my mother. I don't hold any anger toward her anymore. Casey is happily married to a man who would protect her with his dying breath. Mom can't hurt either of us anymore. She'll never have any contact with her grandchildren. And best thing of all is she has to live with her sister."

"Do they not get along?" Megan asked, seeing the mischievous glint in his eyes.

"My aunt makes my mom look like a saint."

Breaking out in laughter, they both jumped in their seat when Marty yelled at them as he was checking out a customer.

"You going to sit there all day, taking up my booth space?"

Both stared of him then looked at the empty booths and broke into laughter again.

Megan decided to put Marty out of his misery and rose from the booth. "I should be going. I need to put my business plan in action. Thank you for lunch. I enjoyed myself."

"That's not fair—I shared with you. At least go out to dinner with me tonight. I promise not to ask any questions."

"I better not." Sadly, she memorized his features, wanting to remember every little detail.

Cole started putting their used wrappers into the plain paper bag the burgers had come in, rising to throw it away. "Why not?"

"Because I'm no angel."

Eight

Holding the paper in hand, Megan peeped through the window, seeing Marty sitting in one of the chairs beside the register. She really, really didn't want to go inside the diner.

There has to be an easier way, she told herself. Darn, she ...

Cutting herself off from saying the same thing, Megan forced herself to push the door open.

The dude didn't bother turning around.

With lagging footsteps, she went to stand next to Marty.

"What you want?"

Yeah, he was going to be as rude today as he was yesterday. She had to take that as a positive sign, or she would shove the pepper shaker where the sun didn't shine.

"I was wondering if I could—"

"Told you yesterday. I'm not hiring." Marty ignored her, turning another page of his newspaper.

"I don't need a job anymore. I went into business for myself. May I put my flyer in your window?"

"Knock yourself out."

Was that a yes or a no? The dude was so mean he could

literally be telling her to knock herself out in response to her question.

"Is that a yes?" she asked hopefully.

Marty looked up at her over his reading glasses. "Kid, you stupid?"

Angrily, she stiffened. "No."

"Then don't act like it. Put the damn thing in the window and get out."

"Don't you want to read it first?"

"Don't have to. You were all over Facebook this morning, promoting your food delivery service."

If Marty had told her he was from Mars, it couldn't be more of a shock.

"You do Facebook?"

Marty got to his feet, wadding the paper into a ball. "Don't worry; I won't be sending you a friend request."

"I didn't expect you would. I just meant ..." she ended lamely.

"I have friends I talk to on Facebook."

Which were probably the only friends the disagreeable man had.

"Have a daughter around your age; helps me keep track of what she's doing."

Marty was full of surprises today. Not only was he sharing that he had a daughter, but he was also talking to her without being outright rude.

"A phone call would do the same."

"Hollis's battleax mother left me when the kid was six years old. By the time I was able to find where she had taken her, Hollis didn't want to hear a thing I had to say."

"I'm sorry you had to go through that. Breakups are hard, especially on children," she sympathized.

"My fault. I should have worn a condom."

And there he was ... the jerk was back.

"You going to order something or not?"

"No." She took the tape out of her pocket and started for the door. "Thanks for letting me place my sign on the window."

"Put the sign up and come back. I'll make you a bag. You can pay me back when you get paid."

"I can't accept—"

"I'm going to put it on the counter. I don't give a fuck if you eat or not," Marty said, going into the back.

Blinking back grateful tears, she went outside to tap her ad on the window. She had made little cutouts on the bottom of the paper. That way, anyone passing by could tear one off.

She stood outside for several minutes once she was done, but finally threw her pride aside and went back in. There, where Marty had been sitting, was a bag of food filled so high that fries were peeking out above, and two sodas.

Megan walked toward the bag and started to pick it up when she decided to sit down and started eating.

While she ate, customers came and went, each time giving her side-eyes that she was brave enough to sit at the counter.

She was thoughtfully eating a French fry when Marty walked out with an order. When the customer left, Marty gave her look of displeasure. "I expected you to go somewhere else to eat."

Megan lifted her chin stubbornly. "Why should I? There's a perfectly good chair here."

"Do what you want," he snapped. "Just don't try to talk my head off. I prefer it quiet."

Bravely, she pulled out another fry. "Marty, I think you're full of hot air."

Marty's beady eyes turned mean.

Her mouth snapped shut when she heard him blast a loud fart. Quickly, she crushed the bag of food closed, picked it up, took her drink, and ran out the door.

Gasping for air outside, through the window, she saw Marty laughing so hard he was bent over the register. Two customers who were waiting outside looked to see what she was staring at.

"What did he do?"

Megan took a step to the side, giving the men room to open the door. Not recognizing one of the men, she assumed he must be new to town.

The man who had spoken, she had to rack her mind to remember who he was. A minute passed before his face clicked into place. Silas Coleman.

The Colemans rarely left their land. To see one was like spotting Bigfoot in the wild. Debating the pros and cons of telling them what Marty had done could hurt business ... or it could help.

She was going to go for the latter.

"He cut gas because I guess I was taking up his counter space."

Both men went to the paper she had just taped to the window, tearing off slips that held her cell phone number.

Silas reached into his back pocket to take out his wallet "I'll give you twenty to go inside and get my order."

The unknown man reached inside his pocket. "I'll give you the same amount if you get mine."

"Hold my stuff." Megan handed Silas her food and drink. Then, taking the money, she took an experimental breath before closing the door behind her. She walked toward the counter and yelled out when Marty didn't come out to see who had entered the restaurant. "I'm here to pick up Silas' and the guy in the suit's order."

She was about to yell again when Marty came out, carrying the orders. His beady eyes followed her movements as she picked up the bags.

"They gonna pay you?"

"They already did," Megan told him, watching for his reaction. It wasn't what she was expecting.

"Good, then you can pay me what you owe me."

She had been excited to have cash again, and it had gone out of her mind that she owed him. Nevertheless, she gave Marty one of her treasured twenties. "Keep the change."

Making a sarcastic face at her, Marty opened the register to take out the change. "Here you go, big spender."

Clenching the bags to her chest, she told herself he wasn't worth going to jail for.

"Don't forget their soda and water."

She moved to the refrigerated cooler on the other side of the register to grab the drinks, aware of Marty watching her.

"Wasn't a terrible idea to place your ad there." Crossing his arms over his chest, he gave her a satisfied grin.

Megan couldn't understand why he seemed so pleased with himself.

"I guess you could say your business is off to a booming start."

The dude had a warped sense of humor.

Megan threw another dirty look at him. "I'd rather have my sense of smell back."

Marty patted his stomach. "Don't worry; it's temporary. I didn't give you a big one."

Why are men so gross? she thought to herself.

Outside, she was handing the men their orders when other customers went past them to head inside the restaurant.

The stranger crossed the street after thanking her, and Silas walked along beside her as they headed toward the parking lot.

"Good to see you back in town."

She found it unusual that Silas was making the effort to be nice to her instead of just taking the food and walking off like the other man. Was he being fake nice? She hadn't even spoken to Silas four times in her whole life. Was this just a ruse? Was Silas trying to find something out to fuel the rumor mill? He would find out she had been overly cautious about everything she had said and done since being back in town.

Unlike big cities, in small towns like Treepoint, people were gauged by their reputation. Hers was in tatters. The finest seamstress in Treepoint couldn't repair the damage she had inflicted on herself.

"Then you're one of the few who thinks that way," Megan replied with resignation.

Silas frowned. "Are the townspeople giving you a hard time?"

Megan stopped in her tracks. No, now that she gave it a thought, they weren't. Everyone she had talked to was polite, except for Chelsea and Marty. Chelsea and she never got along, so there was nothing new about that. Marty was naturally unpleasant to everyone in town—he wasn't making an exception for her.

Megan realized Silas was waiting for her answer.

"No, they aren't," she admitted.

Silas's frown cleared. "It's Christmastime, Megan. 'Tis the season to be jolly. Lighten up, and people around you will, too," Silas advised.

"I will." Seeing his frown back, she laughed. "I will!" she cheerfully promised as she pushed the unlock button on her key fob.

"I'm going to hold you to that."

"Okay." Thinking Silas was joking, Megan teased him back. "You won't catch me with a humbug spirit again."

She had to do a double-take when Silas' expression filled with amusement. She had never considered Silas a handsome man before. When he came to town, people would give the Colemans a wide berth. His inflexible, almost austere attitude made him unapproachable unless he made the first move.

Now, with amusement on his face, Silas seemed almost ... friendly.

"Good. I better be going. The boys are waiting for their food. You take care, Megan."

"You, too, Silas."

As she got in her car, she felt more positive than she had in a long time. Silas was right; she did need to relax more. Be more positive. What could it hurt?

Nine

"Here you go." Megan set Knox's order on his desk.

Pushing his chair closer to the desk, Knox started pulling out his fries and burgers. "I was worried you wouldn't bring the ketchup packets. I know Marty gives you a hard time when you ask for them."

Closing the delivery bag she had invested in to keep the food warm, she watched as Knox devoured his burger in one bite. "Marty and I have come to an understanding."

"Really? What's the arrangement?"

"I buy the ketchup packets, then I can get as many as I need for my customers."

"That asshole could give Greer a lesson on being stingy."

Megan didn't miss the sad way Knox had mentioned Greer.

"How's Greer doing?"

"He still won't leave his house. I told him he could have a desk job until he recovers."

"I take it he told you no."

"He told me to shove the desk up my ass."

Feeling bad for Knox, she opened her bag and took more ketchup packs out, setting them on the corner of his desk.

"I'm sure it's hard for him, not being able to do the physical activities he's used to, especially with him working here."

Knox lifted a curious brow as he reached into the bag. "What do you mean about that? Why especially here?"

Megan gave a one-shoulder shrug and nodded toward the open doorway. "I'd feel self-conscious, too, coming in here, if I were a man. All of your deputies are buff as heck, and you're no slouch, either. Greer Porter is the most prideful man in Treepoint. There's no way he would come back to work here until he's confident of holding his own against the other men."

Knox angrily threw his empty bag into the trash can by his desk. "Fuck, you're right." His expression grew thoughtful. "I'll have to think about it."

"There you go. I'm sure you'll come up with something." She gave him a conspiratorial wink.

"There's more than one way to catch a rabbit."

Knox was still chuckling as she went out the door.

Being back in Treepoint for nearly two weeks now, she had discovered that Knox had a kind heart. The night Chelsea had called the police on her, Knox was extremely professional as she showed him how she had accidentally made the loud sound Chelsea had heard.

"I'll have a chat with Chelsea," he'd said, irritably closing his notepad. "I don't appreciate the sheriff's office being used in an attempt to cause trouble for you. She will be made aware of that fact. Have a good evening, Megan."

Megan still didn't quite believe that Knox had readily accepted her explanation. He, more than anyone else in town, knew of the mental health evaluations she had gone through to earn her release to the supervised house.

Back in her car, she checked to see if there were any new

orders placed as it warmed. Curious, she also looked to see what Knox had given her. She shook her head at the amount and tucked her cell phone holder onto the dashboard.

She drove back across the street and turned the car off, waiting for another order to come in. It was nearing noon, so she was anticipating something coming in soon. Tapping her feet on the floorboards, she pulled a thick blanket she kept in the car over her shoulders.

"This is getting ridiculous," she complained out loud to herself. When she couldn't take it any longer, she threw the blanket off and grabbed her phone. "To hell with this." Jerking herself out the car, she slammed the door shut just to make herself feel better.

Stomping her feet to get rid of the numbness, she pulled the door open so hard it slapped the outside of the building. Then, jerking the door closed, she threw a challenging gaze at Marty when he came from out the kitchen area.

Stomping toward the counter, she plopped herself down on the chair. "I want a damn cup of coffee," she ordered aggressively.

Marty wiped his hands on a dish towel hanging off his shoulder. "Then you can make it your own damn self."

Wanting nothing more than to chuck the heavy metal napkin holder at him, she had to slowly count to ten to get her temper in check before she went behind the counter.

The coffee was still dripping when she noticed an order.

Reading the order, she nearly burned herself when she saw the name on the transaction—Cole.

She set the pot back on the burner and went through the kitchen door, coming to standstill.

Marty was sitting on a chair with his legs on another, his face twisted in a grimace of pain.

"Are you all right?"

"What in the fuck do you want now?"

Realizing the amount of pain Marty was in, Megan finally got why he didn't want many customers inside the restaurant. Customers had to be waited on, and Marty was clearly not capable of waiting on a large quantity of tables. She didn't have to wonder why Marty didn't hire additional help, either. Greer wasn't the only one in town who had a huge ego.

"I need two grand bags with extra fries."

Hiding her sympathy, Megan went back to the front of the restaurant. Drinking her coffee, she looked at the address for Cole's order.

"Darn," she muttered under her breath.

"What in the fuck is wrong?" was yelled out from the kitchen.

Any sympathy she felt for Marty went up in smoke.

What the heck? How had he heard her?

Pivoting in her chair, she scrutinized the walls and tables. He had to be rec—

Unable to spot a camera, she was about to give up when something told her to look up. And there it was ... in the light fixture. He didn't need the bell; the camera was doing all the work. Why in the heck would Marty have to go to such an extreme to record his customers?

A sick thought entered her mind.

She jumped off the stool and went to the restroom, checking for cameras there. When she came out, Marty was leaning against the counter of the cash register.

"Find what you were looking for?" he asked drily.

Megan felt the riding-high flush flood her cheeks. Since he had figured out what she was doing, Megan saw no sense in mincing words.

"Why do you have cameras with recording devices in your lights?"

Marty made a sarcastic face at her. "You have to ask me that?"

"Obviously, or I wouldn't have asked."

"You think I'm looking down woman's tops?"

"I think that's a possibility."

"I don't get off looking down women's tops."

Megan didn't want to believe he did, but unless he came up with a better excuse as to what was going on, she would have to go with that thought.

"Then why?"

"I have made a few enemies in my lifetime. For some reason, people don't like me. I figured if someone comes in to kill me, the least the fucker could do is tell me why he's going kill me. That way, it'll be on tape. I don't want the fucker to get away."

"Oh ..." She nodded in understanding. That people hated Marty enough to kill him ... *that* she could believe.

Ten

Nervous, Megan pulled into The Last Riders' parking lot. Her nerves didn't settle at the thought of seeing Cole.

She parked her car and got out, taking her delivery bag. To calm her nerves, she started singing a song in her head. Music always soothed her or allowed her to escape to someone else's heartache. Mentally singing "Jingle Bells," she cautiously walked to where Cole and another man were working on a bike.

"Hey!" Cole greeted her with an infectious grin.

"Hey." More soberly, she walked up to the two men. "How's it going?"

"Could be better." Glaring at the motorcycle in frustration, the other man dropped a tool he was using into a toolbox below.

"Could be worse," Cole countered.

"Not by much. The motor's blown. I've put so much money into this bike already, I could have bought a brand-new one."

"I can't argue with that." Taking the bags she had picked

up out, Cole nodded his head in the other man's direction. "Moon, meet Megan. Megan, this a friend of mine, Moon," Cole introduced.

"Hi, Moon." Not recognizing him, she stopped singing "Jingle Bells," relaxing at the friendly smile Moon gave her.

"Nice to meet you." Moon threw a leg over his motorcycle to sit as he took one of the bags from Cole. "So, you the one who's brave enough to deal with fartface?"

Megan crinkled her nose at the term. "I take it I wasn't the only one nuked by his fart bombs?"

"Put it this way ..." Moon's grim demeanor showed the graphic language which was about to be used.

"I don't want to hold Megan up," Cole interrupted. "I'm sure she has other deliveries to make." Shoving his bag into Moon's hands, Cole started propelling her away from him. "Let me walk you to your car."

A warm glow filled her at the way Cole took charge, leading her away before Moon could start ranting about Marty.

"I guess your new business is booming?" Cole asked humorously.

"I'm staying busy," she agreed with a shy glance as he opened the car door for her.

As she got in, Cole positioned himself so his body would block her from closing the door. "Too busy to take a day off?"

"Cole ..." Staring at his face, she almost broke. She jerked her gaze away to look at the house above and told him, "I can't. You're going to be leaving after Christmas—"

"Christmas is two and half weeks away."

"Let me finish. I've never been good at making friends—they end up hating me." She could tell he wanted to interrupt her again yet was respectfully listening.

Men never listened to her. They would either completely

ignore what she was saying, overtalk her, or the worst—they would gaslight her.

"I think you would make a wonderful friend, so wonderful, in fact, that when our friendship ended, I'm afraid it might affect me finally getting my life back on track. Mentally, I can't afford any more mistakes." As she glanced back at him, the warm glow turned into the comforting warmth of a fireplace, just enough to feel the heat without getting burned.

"I'm not the same man I was before having my brain scrambled, nor the child-man I was after. What you're looking at is a born-again man who just wants to explore a connection I felt when we rescued that cat together. In other words, to make my meaning clearer, I was trying to ask you out on a date. Unless you didn't feel the same connection?"

"I did," she admitted, blushing. "I just can't take a chance."

"All right. I don't want to push you into going out with me. There are almost three weeks left before I leave; you might change your mind. Unless the reason you don't want to go out with me is because you think I'm too old for you?"

"I married a man older than you."

"Then I guess I don't need to be worried about that being a problem."

"Cole, you're perfect in every way." Megan felt her cheeks burning hotter. "The problem is me."

"My sister would pass out if she heard you say I was perfect."

"Tell me one thing you're bad at."

"Talking you into going out with me."

Was he really giving her puppy eyes?

The sound of her cell phone alerting an order had been placed made her tear her gaze away.

"I have to go."

"See you soon." Cole moved to the side of the door. "Watch your hand."

He closed the door when she moved her hand away. The simple gentlemanly gesture caused all the warmth she had been building inside give her an emotional high, as if she were riding in a hot air balloon and it was going so high she could look down on this marvelous scenery she had never been able to see before.

It's going to burst, a whisper warned from the back of her mind.

Not this time, Megan shushed the negative thought before it could gain ground.

She started swaying in her seat. "*Jingle bells ...*"

Eleven

He has to be kidding, right?

Blowing a wayward hair away from the corner of her mouth, Megan plunked her cell phone onto the counter.

"Who in the hell pissed in your coffee?"

"Quit watching me," Megan snapped. She placed the orders Marty had just completed into her delivery bag, then filled a thermos with hot coffee. Satisfied everything was ready to go, she was resolved to come to a mutual agreement about the camera-watching. "Why do you enjoy being so obnoxious?"

"Misery loves company." Marty scooted the chair his leg was propped on closer so he could massage his swollen calf.

"Let me see." She moved nearer and attempted to lift the bottom of his jogging pants.

"Fuck off."

"Am I expected to watch you suffer without doing anything to help?"

"You really want to help?" Marty asked in a sweet tone she hadn't heard from him before.

Sincerely, she placed a hand on his shoulder. "Yes, I do."

"Then go deliver that fucking food before it gets cold and leave me the fuck alone!" he bellowed.

She bent over to yell in his face. "See if I care anymore. I hope your foot rots off, you mean asshole." With that, she stormed out of the restaurant,

She had to turn the radio on. Marty made her so furious that the only song she wanted to sing was "Kung Fu Fighting," making karate chopping motions with her hands as she pretended to karate chop Marty in her imagination. She was in a much lighter mood when she arrived at her first stop.

"Why did I take this order?" she muttered under her breath as she sloughed through the un-shoveled snow to the hotel office door.

Money. Car repairs were eating up her profits. She needed to buy a car, or her new business would go under.

When she opened the door, she cheered up at seeing Chelsea wasn't working behind the counter.

"Thank goodness. I'm starving."

"How are you doing today, Harford?" she greeted him warmly.

The day clerk was an older man, retired, who actually lived in Jamestown. Megan had met him when she came to the office to extend her stay. Since she'd learned that Chelsea worked at night and days on the weekends, any reasons she needed to go to the office were taken care of when Harford was working.

"You bring the extra pickles I asked for?"

"Of course."

Marty had argued, right up until she promised to give him a dollar for them.

"Then it's a great day."

She handed Harford the food and gave him a puzzled look. "I thought you didn't work on the weekends?"

"The owner of the hotel asked me to take Chelsea's shift so they could have a meeting. Chelsea had to drive to Jamestown for the convo, so I'm guessing I'll be stuck here for another hour or two."

"Ah … Well, that explains that," she joked, giving him a jaunty wave goodbye. "Drive safe on your way home."

"Will do."

In a better frame of mind, Megan drove off in the direction of the Coleman's property. The roads were clear as she drove up the steep mountain. Thankfully, there was a guardrail. Still, her worst nightmare would be to find herself in a skid and go over the edge. Many out-of-town visitors would travel this route to Virginia. The curvy two-lane road was deceptively innocuous if you stayed within the speed limit. Unfortunately, less cautious drivers found the low speed limit was there for a reason at a cost.

She almost missed the turnoff for the Coleman's, but saw it in the nick of time. Megan didn't know what to expect because she hadn't been up here since she was a child. At the end of the driveway stood a beautiful older home.

Grabbing her delivery bag, she got out of the car and headed for the front door of the picturesque home.

A loud whistle to the side the house made her turn.

"Over here!"

Spotting Matthew Coleman, Silas's brother, waving, Megan started walking in his direction, admiring the woodsy property instead of gawking at Matthew's bare chest.

As she neared the metal building where Matthew was, she nearly dropped the delivery bag when Cole and another Coleman brother strode out to wait for her.

She gathered her composure at the wall of masculinity that would have the Chippendale dancers reaching for their shirts, she said a silent prayer not to make a fool of herself. Racking her brain, she was able to recall Issac's name.

Silas had six younger brothers and two sisters. One had been killed in an accident with their father. It was one of the saddest memories she could vividly recall—attending Leah's graveside funeral. Her family had been one of the few to attend the service.

"Good afternoon, Megan," Issac greeted her.

"Hi, Issac, how are all of you doing?" She became nervous under Cole's scrutiny.

"Hungry enough to eat Silas' leftover meatloaf if you didn't get here so quickly." He grinned. "Silas is a good cook, but he loves to experiment with his meatloaf recipes." Issac made a disgusted face. "They're getting worse instead of better."

Matthew stepped forward to take the order from her. "You're welcome to stay and sit a spell." he offered. "We have plenty of food if you're hungry."

"Thanks, but I better head back to town," she refused.

After thanking her, Matthew and Issac moved toward to a wooden picnic table beside the building they had come out of.

Instead of going with the brothers, Cole fell in step with her. "How's your day going?" he asked casually.

"Pretty much the same as yesterday." Unable to hold her curiosity at bay any longer, she gave Cole a fleeting glance. "A little chilly for what you're wearing."

"Matthew and Issac are teaching me how to work their forge."

"I bet that's interesting."

"For the first ten minutes, then it becomes a sauna. You saved me; I needed an excuse to escape."

"What about your shirt?" Hearing the breathlessness in her voice, she smacked the delivery bag against the side of her leg.

Confusion marred his expression as they reached her car. "You usually leave your engine running?"

"Depends. I need a new starter. If the weather is above sixty degrees, she'll start right up. If it dips below, I have to jump her. For the next few days, I should be good. I'm just holding off putting more money into this one. I almost have enough to get a used car."

"I don't like the idea of you being out in this car if it isn't reliable." Frowning, he opened the door for her. "I could lend you the mon—"

"No, thank you. I'm doing dandy."

"I take it you're a fan of Dolly's?"

"Fooorrrreeveerr," she quipped, tossing the delivery bag like a frisbee into the back of the car.

"I happen to have an extra ticket for the Christmas fair tonight. We could do dinner first then go to the fair afterward." His eyes twinkled in merriment. "Of course, I'd drive."

"Sorry, I have to work. Bye, Cole." She practically threw herself in the front seat, then shut the door before he had a chance to react. Megan felt bad for ditching him so fast.

Cole standing there, bare-chested, with nipples taut from the cold air was more than she could physically take. Her hands were shaking on the steering wheel as she backed up into the side section of gravel. Cutting the wheels, she turned the car in the other direction to head down the long driveway. What made it worse was Cole knew the effect his body was having on her.

Oh yes, he did ... Pfft... she could see the naughty gleam in his eyes. She deserved a damn medal for the way she had restrained herself.

Curt was the only man she'd had sex with, and to be honest, before meeting Cole, she hadn't planned to experience it with another. Yet, the more she was around him, the more she had to restrain herself from touching him. He was like catnip. All she had to do was catch a whiff, and her stagnant libido went haywire.

Dammit, there was a pill for everything. There should be a pill you could take to stop you from being attracted to someone with the potential to wreck your sanity. She would take it ... the darn thing didn't even have to be FDA approved. She would take a chance, you betcha. She would risk taking an experimental drug any day of the week and twice on Sunday rather than trust her own judgment with Cole.

"You've got this, Megan. You can do this," she reassured herself. All she had to do was stay away from him until after Christmas. "You said this before." Megan didn't appreciate how snide her subconscious sounded.

Her subconscious flipped her off.

"I'm going to keep saying it until you finally listen."

Megan shot Cole a dirty look as the door closed. Fuming, she stomped her boots on the welcome mat before approaching the counter of the gas station as the clerk finished waiting on a customer and thrust the order at Cole's stomach. He caught the bag and gave her an innocent grin.

"What are you doing here?" she hissed at him under her breath.

Cole quirked an eyebrow at her. "This is a gas station."

"I know that," she snapped. "I didn't see your car at the pumps."

"I walked over here after the fair. Casey and Max are still there with the kids. They're going to pick me up on the way back."

"That still doesn't explain why you walked all the way here." Tapping one of her boots, she waited to hear what possible explanation Cole could up with to warrant a two-mile walk.

"Oh ... I'm sorry." He handed the bag of food to the amused clerk, who was watching them. "Megan, this is Joel—"

"We've met. This is the only gas station in town."

Joel burst out laughing while unpacking his food. "Perhaps you better tell her, Cole, before those boots start walking."

Cole didn't look perturbed, giving her the same gentle smile he always gave her. "I come here regularly. Like you said, it's the only gas station in town," he said wryly, letting her know he hadn't missed the irritation she hadn't attempted to hide. "The last time I was in here, Joel noticed I was driving a rental car and told me he had a car for sale. I didn't have the time to check it out then, so I decided to walk over here after the fair and see if it would work for me."

The explanation sounded reasonable to her, but she still didn't believe him.

"Does it?"

"I wanted it to since the price is so low. I could park it at The Last Riders' and be able to drive when I visit. I decided against buying it, though. It's a tad bit small for me." Cole shrugged. "Then I remembered you mentioned having car trouble. I would have called or texted you, but you're not accepting either."

"I wonder why," she said through tight lips.

Cole cleared his throat. "Anyway, I told Joel you might be interested. He came up with the idea of ordering food since he's hungry. 'Kill to two birds with one stone' kind of thing."

"Oh ..." Her irritation drew the word out longer than necessary. "I think it was meant to take out one bird for you, too."

"Could be."

How was she was supposed to stay angry at him when he was so adorably maddening?

Exasperated, she looked at Joel to see he had finished and

was tossing the bag in the trash. "How much is the car?" There was no need to look at the car if the price was out of her range.

Joel cracked his knuckles, as if he was preparing to barter. "Three thousand, but it's worth five. Plus, I put on brand-new tires, wipers, and did a fluid check. She's raring to go."

"I have a few minutes to spare. Where's the car?"

"Cole, you mind showing her? I can't leave the register."

"Not at all."

The men shared triumph grins, as if she weren't watching.

"How am I not surprised?" Shaking her head at the two nuts, she followed Cole outside.

"This is it." Using a gloved hand, Cole brushed away a thin layer of snow. "What do you think?"

"I think it looks too good to be true."

"I drove it around town; the only problem for me was leg room." Cole reached into his pocket and pulled out a key. "You want to take a test drive?"

"Yes." She took the key and opened the door, then watched as Cole went to stand by the ice machine. Something about the expectant way he stood, waiting for her to drive off without him, hurt a part of her that she didn't know could still be touched. "Aren't you coming?"

His smile lit up his whole face.

Megan felt a tingling pain in her lower stomach, as if some mysterious force was playing pinball with her ovaries.

"Go ahead and get in. I need to check if any orders are pending." She raised her cell phone and stared at the dark screen until Cole was inside. Waiting a mere second after hearing the door shut, Megan laid her face on the roof, expecting steam to rise. She blinked falling snowflakes off her lashes to clear her vision.

How was she supposed to resist him? He was the Christmas wish she had asked Santa for after watching an animated movie where the prince had swept the beautiful girl off her feet to make her his princess. She had believed in that fairy tale until Curt gave her a dose of reality and showed her that fairy tales, tooth fairies, and Santa didn't exist.

Tonight, standing in the light of the gas station, with snowflakes glistening in his blond hair, and true happiness glinting in his eyes, Cole had restored that cherished childhood belief.

Santa did exist.

Twelve

"Are you warm enough?" Cole asked solicitously. "You don't need to turn the heat up higher?"

"No!" Megan quickly lowered the volume of her voice at realizing how loud it sounded in the car. "I'm comfortable."

"What do you think?"

She refrained from sharing the inappropriate thoughts swirling through her mind and focused on the car instead. "Joel must have babied this car. It drives like a dream. It handles much better on the roads than mine."

"I'm glad you like it. Are you going to buy it?"

"I want to. I'll ask Joel if he'll give me a couple of weeks to come up with the money."

"I could—"

"No, thanks. If Joel can't wait, then I'll find another car."

Megan felt Cole's eyes on her profile in the dark.

"Or I could lend you the money."

"Thanks, but no. I appreciate the offer."

Megan heard Cole's heavy sigh and saw him twisting in his seat to face her.

"You're a very stubborn woman. Do you think I would expect something from you if I lend you the money?"

Dammit, did he have to sound so darn hurt?

"I truly appreciate your offer. I know you mean well. It's just ... I want to prove ..." Megan tightened her grip on the steering wheel. When she turned down a connecting side street, she caught a glimpse of his face in the light of the streetlamp.

He was worried about her car breaking down. She wasn't being fair to him, nor herself. He was too good of a person for her to continue to let him believe she was worthy of being his friend, much less starting a relationship with.

"Cole, there's no way you'll be able to convince me you haven't heard about me."

"I don't listen to gossip."

"Depends on who told you if it was gossip or not."

When Cole remained silent, a dull pain start started in the pit of her stomach, extending upward toward the region of her heart.

"I get it. Too many to say? Don't worry; I won't ask who. I should have told you myself." She shrugged. "Lord knows I gave them plenty to talk about."

"I don't take into account what people say about other people. I like to form my own opinion."

"You're starting to sound more Kentuckian every day." She laughed.

Cole laughed, too. "I found out the first time I came here. Last year, after I went back to Texas, it took me a good month to lose the accent."

Megan turned serious. "I'll never be able to lose the accent."

"I don't want you to. I like it."

"When I was younger, I would watch YouTube videos on how to get rid of your accent." Megan gave a short, bitter laugh. "My husband would make fun of me. He told me I couldn't make a purse out of a sow's ear." She cut the wheels to drive back down the main drag of town. "When I told you I had married someone older than you, you weren't surprised."

"No."

Megan nodded at Cole admitting the truth. "I like that you don't lie to me. That's all my husband ever did—lie after lie. But you want to know the sickest part?"

"No," he replied softly, turning more fully toward her to brace his long arm on her seat. "But if you want to talk, I can listen."

"You don't want all the sordid details of my marriage? At one time, I couldn't walk down the sidewalk without someone asking me about Curt."

"What was the sickest part of his lies?"

"Could you turn the heat up? I'm starting to get cold."

Cole leaned forward to tap a button, increasing the heat.

"The sickest part was I knew what was coming out of his mouth was lies."

"Before you married him?"

"Yes." She turned down another neighborhood.

"Then why did you marry him? Did you think you could change him?"

"No. Curt was never going to change, and he certainly didn't care about me enough to make the effort."

Leaving the neighborhood, she went straight, then cut down another street. She passed the back of the church before she pulled into the parking lot, where she braked and put the car in *Park*.

"You're the first person to ask me why I married Curt, did you know that?" Megan stared sightlessly at the plot of land next to the church playground. The headlights from the car illuminated the untouched beauty of the newly falling snow.

"Several people tried to talk me out of marrying him, but none of them asked me why."

"You don't have to answer if you don't want to."

Megan bent her head, hating herself. "I don't want you to look down on me," she whispered.

Cole's hand left the back of her seat to slide around her shoulders while his other hand went under her chin to lift her head and turn it so she was staring directly at him. "I could never look down on you, whatever you tell me." Cupping her face, he leaned forward to brush a soft kiss across her forehead. "If talking about your husband is making you upset, we can wait. There's no rush." Cole nodded his head sideways. "How good are you at making a snowman?"

"I've never made one," she confessed.

"I bet I can make one better than you."

Giving a shaky laugh, she reached into her coat pocket to take out her gloves. She cut the engine, then gave him a competitive smile. "I'll take that bet."

They got out of the car and ran toward the empty lot.

Megan watched Cole gather snow to form a snowball then roll it across the ground to make the ball grow bigger and copied his actions.

"Joel will think I've stolen his car," she said only half-jokingly.

"No, I'll text him."

She continued to work on her snowman as Cole text Joel, then compared hers to his. It was pathetic. She was still rolling her base, while Cole was forming his second snowball. Rolling the sleeves of her jacket up, she pushed the snowball harder, making it bigger. Satisfied, she started on her second snowball.

"Joel said it's cool. If the station is closed when we get back, he told me to leave the key under the mat. I told him I'd give you his number so you can talk to him about buying the car."

"That was nice of him."

"He is," Cole agreed, lifting his second ball onto the base. "Not as nice as me. He doesn't give free refills."

Giggling at the aggrieved tone in Cole's voice, she pushed her second snowball over to her base. On her second attempt of lifting it, she found it pulled out of her hands and placed on the base.

"We're making a regular snowman, not the abominable one."

Megan stepped back to study hers. "I thought mine was the same size of yours. I might have miscalculated a tad bit."

"A tad?" Cole laughed, shaking his head. "Yours is twice the size of mine."

"At least the head will be small. I'll be able to lift it. I don't want you to think I cheated with you doing half the work."

Cole went back to working on his snowman. "You worry about the strangest things."

Megan straightened from rolling her snowball. Cole was right; she did worry too much. She was constantly nit-picking everything she said and did.

Promising herself to stop worrying over every little thing, she concentrated on beating Cole.

Once she had all three snowballs in place, she started searching for objects to use as decorations. She had no problem finding the sticks for arms. Then she found some small gravel to make a mouth and eyes. Taking off her scarf, she wounded it around the snowman then topped it off with her hat.

The snowmen looked similar, other than size. Cole had used a cap for his snowman and gravel to decorate with. Both then started searching for a nose. Whoever came up the better option would basically win the contest.

Using her foot to kick at the frozen gravel, Megan didn't look up when she heard a vehicle speed down the street. She was far enough off the road that she wasn't worried about getting hit, nor did she worry about Cole, as he was near the church dumpster, even farther away from the road.

Listening to the vehicle approach, she jerked her head up at the sound of it accelerating. Until it was almost upon her, she couldn't make out the truck's color .

As she watched, she knew they were going to hit her. Whoever was driving had turned the wheels to go off the road toward where she was standing.

She closed her eyes and thought about how she wasn't even going to have time to say goodbye to Cole.

A sudden gasp escaped her when strong arms lifted her, pressing her tightly against a warm body. When she opened her eyes, Cole's furious eyes caught hers as he launched them away from the road.

"What the hell? You didn't even try to dodge that maniac. You stood there like a sitting duck!"

Finding herself lying on the snow-covered ground with Cole glaring at her furiously, she brushed the clump of snow off the back of his shoulders from when their bodies had inadvertently tackled his snowman.

"I thought he would swerve away from me," she lied. "Whoever it was must have been drunk."

Rolling off her, Cole sat up and took his cell phone out of his pocket.

"Who are you calling?" She sat up next to him and watched as he pressed a button on his cell phone.

"Knox. He needs to know some maniac nearly killed you."

Megan reached out, disconnecting the call. "Where's your Christmas spirit?"

"It was knocked out of me when you were almost mowed down."

"Will it come back if I agree to go on a date with you?"

What if the driver hadn't been drunk but had been a Last

Rider, bent on revenge? She didn't want Cole to make himself a target trying to protect her.

Cole sent her a penetrating stare. "Why don't you want me to call Knox?"

"Leave it alone, Cole. Please. Do you not want to go out with me anymore?"

"You know I do, which is why you're using it as a bargaining chip. I'll leave it alone," he said firmly, showing he wasn't as easily malleable as she'd assumed. "But if I see any more shady shit happening around you, I'm calling Knox."

"You won't have to. I'll call him myself."

He lifted her up and started brushing the snow off her legs and arms. "When do you want to go out?"

"I think tomorrow is going to be busy. Mondays have been slow. We could go somewhere then?"

"Okay. Any place you want to go in particular?"

"Do you mind if we go someplace out of town? You can choose. I'm pretty flexible where food is concerned. I can eat anything."

"Then leave it to me. I know of the perfect place."

She wasn't worried. The only exotic food within a fifty-mile radius was the Italian pizza joint in Jamestown.

Finished brushing her off, Cole went to remove her hat and scarf from the snowman. "I guess you won." He gave her a pitiful pout then wrapped the scarf back around her and sweetly slid the cap back on, tucking stray hairs inside. He was standing so close that she had to tilt her head back.

"Do you actually think I won't accept the win because of your boyish charm? I was going to win, anyway." She was about to *pfft* him when he gave her a seductive smile. If she weren't wearing boots, it would have melted the snow beneath her.

"Why not? It was good enough to convince you to let me take the drive test with you."

Thirteen

⟨⟨~∽⟩⟩

Thankfully, the automatic doors slid open as she approached the entrance. She had held it together when she went to see Viper. *This is just another test I have to pass*, Megan told herself.

Delivery bag in hand, she passed the reception desk and walked through the empty lobby to the bank of elevators, behind a small grouped sitting area, then pressed the elevator button. The sound of tinkling water was new. She located the sound on a nearby wall near another sitting area. She then turned to find the elevator door had opened. Only through sheer force of will did she manage to step inside and push the button she needed.

"You've got this, Megan," she assured herself in the empty elevator. "You handled nearly being run over like a champ, so this will be a piece of cake.

She stepped out onto the third floor and moved down the familiar hallway until she came to the office she wanted. Repeating the same assurances in her head, she knocked on the door.

"Come in."

She wanted to puke but went inside.

"Ah ... You're here," Dr. Price greeted her cordially from behind his desk. "You're a lifesaver."

She opened her insulated bag and took out Dr. Price's order. Remembering Silas' advice, Megan allowed herself to crack a smile. "Glad to help."

Standing, Dr. Price came around his desk to take the food "I'm happy to see you're back in town. I don't have to ask how you're doing—you look amazing."

She had anticipated her hot air balloon to be shot into smithereens, yet Dr. Price turned what could have been an uncomfortable situation into an opportunity to become reacquainted with an old friend.

"Thank you. You don't look too bad yourself."

"I try." Giving her a wink, he patted his stomach under his white coat. "I've been on a diet, which I'm getting ready to ditch, thanks to your delivery service. It isn't easy being stuck in the hospital fourteen hours a day. Sometimes, I just need a good hamburger to remind me what normal food tastes like."

"The cafeteria food isn't too bad."

Dr. Price grimaced as he sat back down. "Some days are better than others."

"Do they still serve chicken pot pie on Wednesday?"

"No, they moved it to Saturday, my day off. Wednesday is beef stroganoff. I was considering changing schedules until I found out Treepoint has a delivery driver courageous enough to face the dreaded Marty, who has made mincemeat out of those who have tried before. How are you liking being a delivery driver, by the way?"

"What's not to like?" She shrugged lightly. "I get to be my own boss."

"That's always a plus. It's been nice seeing you again."

She bit her lip. Her nervousness had been put at ease by his relaxed attitude, allowing her concern to migrate from herself to someone else.

"Could I bother you for a couple of minutes? I'm worried about something, and I don't know what to do."

Dr. Price gave her encouraging smile. "Of course. Go ahead."

"I have a ... friend..." Calling Marty a friend was a stretch, but she didn't think it was her place to talk about him without his permission. "He isn't able to stand on his feet for long, and I can tell he's in a lot of pain. Is there something I can do to help him?"

"Other than offering assistance, I'm afraid not. Your friend doesn't want to seek medical advice?"

"Nooo ... he's not exactly receptive to any advice, medical or not."

Dr. Price raised his eyebrows in cynical amusement. "Believe me; when the pain gets bad enough, he will become more receptive to medical advice."

Megan felt a wave of sadness when the Dr. Price's expression turned defeated.

"Unfortunately, by then, many times, it will be too late. All you can to do is keep attempting to talk some sense into him."

"I will. I appreciate you taking the time out of your busy schedule to answer my question."

"Anytime. I'm willing to answer any question whenever you're ready for me to."

Sensitive to the meaning Dr. Price was trying to impart without saying so, Megan took the plunge into the murky waters of her past self. There was only one question burning in her mind that she hadn't been ready for the answer. If she couldn't handle it when she was in the best mindset of her life, she never would.

Shoving her hand into her pocket, she stared out the

window, watching people come and go to and from their cars. "Was it my fault my baby died?"

"No. None of it was your fault. You went into premature labor. No one can say for sure why these things happen. You kept your prenatal appointments faithfully. My grandfather told me you would write questions to ask him in a notebook you would bring to your appointments."

"I didn't want to forget anything important." Her voice came out whisper thin.

"You were working not only to support yourself and your baby, but also Curt, who could have taken some off the pressure off you instead of compounding it. There wasn't a person in town who didn't see or hear how he treated you. Then, when anyone would try to step in, you would act blasé about the ugly way he behaved."

"My therapist told me I was in a toxic relationship with Curt."

Dr. Price made a disgusted sound. "Megan, your relationship with Curt went beyond toxic to downright mental abuse. My grandfather retired the day after he delivered your baby. He told me, in all the years he had been an obstetrician, never once had he treated a mother who was so harshly handled. My grandfather is the gentlest man I know, yet I had to pull him off Curt in the hallway after hearing Curt telling you he was leaving you."

Megan stoically stood there, gazing out the window, dry-eyed. She had cried too many tears while replaying that memory.

"You didn't deserve that. No woman does."

"I did," she argued hoarsely. "I deserved everything he said."

"Why, Megan? Why?" Dr. Price pleaded with her. "So many people tried to help you, yet you pushed them away. I heard the authorities question if Curt had sexual contact with you when you were in middle school. He had a history of sexual violence—"

Megan spun on her heel angrily. "Which they did nothing about! Then they came to me, expecting me to stick my neck out to be humiliated like the girl he victimized." Megan stared at him in cynical amusement. "No one cared because she was the daughter of the town drunk. Let's be real. Jo was poor; it was only when she hooked up with a man who had money that anyone gave a damn. And then"—she gave a harsh laugh —"they couldn't do a damn thing."

"Yet you came back Treepoint," Dr. Price stated. "Why? You could have gone anywhere; why here?"

"Because I have something to prove!"

Sympathetically, Dr. Price shook his head. "You don't have to prove anything to anyone in this town."

"I have to prove I'm not going to lose my shit again!" Megan smacked a hand over her heart. "I have to know I won't hurt a child again!" Beseechingly, she took a step forward, sinking down onto the lone chair in his office. She clenched her hands into fists and held them on her lap, digging her nails into her palms. "I need to know before I can become involved in a relationship, have children. What if I make friends with someone who has children? Should they be scared of me? You see people on television who attempt to kidnap children, confused the same way I was."

"You won't," he assured her.

"I can't be sure. You can't be sure ..." Begging him with her eyes, Megan dug her nails in deeper.

Dr. Price opened a drawer in his desk to pull a file out. Laying it down, he then placed his folded hands on top. "You have to trust my professional opinion on some level, or you wouldn't have asked my advice for your friend. Do you agree?"

"I do."

"Then this is my medical opinion." Dr. Price's entire

visage changed, turning from relaxed and confiding to professional and matter of fact. "Megan, you had a psychotic break, which was brought on by the trauma of losing your child, your husband leaving you, the financial distress this caused, and I also believe your husband was emotionally abusive during your pregnancy. Not only did you suffer those stressors, you were also prescribed pain medication.

"My grandfather left instructions for you to be monitored closely. He was finishing his report when Curt came out of your room. My grandfather confronted him, which turned physical. Medical personnel immediately broke them apart. By then, it was too late. My grandfather had a heart attack during the altercation. Personnel, who should have been watching, unintentionally left you unattended when they had to rush granddad to the ICU.

"You should never have been able to reach the nursey. You continuously asked to hold your deceased child, and Curt refused your request repeatedly. It is believed you went in search of your daughter to hold her. Unfortunately, you found the nursery. In my medical opinion—and several others, I might add—seeing the James' baby in the incubator was more than you, in your highly emotional state, could handle. I don't know if many women in the same set of circumstances, in the exact same set of emotional turmoil, wouldn't have broken under that pressure, and I'm not taking into account"—he opened the folder and took out a piece of paper, laying it on the desk for her to see—"you were just eighteen years old."

Unclenching her fists, she picked up the paper, which was a photocopy of her driver's license. God, the full reality of just how young she had been struck her. At that age, she had thought herself more mature looking. How many times had Curt told her she didn't look her age? That she appeared more mature than other girls her age?

Teardrops splattered on the thin piece of paper she was

holding. There was nothing mature about the girl, not the clothes she was wearing, the makeup applied with a teen's heavy hand, nor the frightened way she looked at the camera.

Dr. Price pushed the file toward her. "My grandfather made photocopies of your file in case you wanted to sue. He mailed it to you several times, but you kept sending it back."

Megan didn't reach for the file. "I was afraid."

"Why?"

"I was afraid it would show I was the one responsible for my child's death."

"Yet you just asked."

Megan gave him a wry smile. "I figured if I flipped out again, you would know what to do. You would just get me readmitted to the mental care hospital Curt sent me to before."

Dr. Price scowled. "I would never have sent you to the place Curt had you committed to."

"I don't understand why not. Innova Wellness Hospital treated me extremely well. I was completely—"

Megan broke off when Dr. Price started shaking his head.

"Curt had you committed to Revital Mental Hospital. Basically, it has ..."

"Tell me," Megan urged. She could see he was hesitant about what to tell her.

"Let me put it this way: Revital patients are mainly kept sedated, not treated."

Why was she not surprised?

"Then how do I not remember Revital?"

"In all likelihood, it's due to the medication you were prescribed there."

"So, Curt must have seen the hospital wasn't good and had me moved." That did surprise her. At least Curt had done one good thing for her before he died.

Again, Dr. Price shook his head. "Curt wasn't the one

who had you moved. Winter James hired Diamond Bates to take over your guardianship."

"The sheriff's wife?"

"Yes. After Curt's death, Winter James contacted your parents and asked them to assign Diamond guardianship. The Last Riders also agreed to pay any medical and living costs you needed until you were able to manage on your own."

It was a good thing she was sitting.

Megan buried her face in her hands. "I thought they wanted to kill me," she sobbed. Then, gathering herself, she wiped her tears away.

"What I told you is common knowledge. Around that time, your parents must have told some of their friends in town, and gossip spread. I would hazard to guess the James aren't ready to be buddy-buddy with you, but I suspect Winter had more to do with it than Viper. She's selfless where her students are concerned."

Her eyes shied away from his. "Mrs. James is a woman I could never be in a million years."

"Nor could Winter ever be like you."

Megan gave an ironic laugh. "That's for sure."

"Ah ... you're missing my point."

"That's where *you're* wrong." Megan stood and moved to where she had left the delivery bag sitting by the window. "I do get your point. Everyone's different—I get that. Let me rephrase what I said. Mrs. James is the type of woman I could never be. Mrs. James proves she's selfless every day. She's a prominent member of Treepoint's community. I could walk out this door and stop the first person I come to and ask what selfless act she has done for them. However, if I asked the same person about me"—Megan placed her hand on her chest—"they would laugh their head off. I've taken care of Megan first when I've been put to the test. I really dislike that about myself —I really do. I've been working to change that characteristic about myself, but even if I succeed, I would never be able to reach the level of Mrs. James."

Seeing Dr. Price was going to argue further, she gestured to his food sitting uneaten on his desk. "I'm going to refund you the money for your food. I'm sure it's ice-cold by now." Moving to the door, she called out over her shoulder, "Have a good one!"

As she left the hospital, she didn't hear a single "Jingle Bells" in her head like she had when she arrived. Other lyrics came to her mind, slower, which would keep her in the holiday mood. She hummed "Hard Candy Christmas" as she took out her phone in her car to refund Dr. Price's order.

Dolly had the right idea. She wasn't going to let past sorrow ruin her holiday. She had looked forward to tomorrow's date with Cole all day. Her balloon had weathered the dark skies with Dr. Price. It had been a shaky journey, but it survived. All in all, it had been an okay day. Her sanity survived intact.

Megan stopped humming.

"You know, Dolly, suddenly, I'm in the mood for a candy bar."

Fourteen

wkwardly, Megan waited outside her hotel room for
Cole to arrive. She had spent a restless night arguing
with herself on whether to cancel their date, aware
it wasn't the responsible thing to do, considering she was still
getting on her feet and there might have been an attempt on
her life. After replaying what Dr. Price had revealed to her the
day before about The Last Riders, however, she no longer
believed they wanted payback. Whoever had nearly struck her
must have been coming from Mick's or overindulged at a
Christmas party.

A gust of cold wind made her shiver, and she was about to
head back inside to wait, when a black truck pulling into the
back entrance of the hotel caught her attention.

The size and shape of the truck were the same as the one
that had almost mowed her over.

Staying where was, she watched as it drove past her to the
front of the hotel. She was only able to catch a fleeting glance
of the man and woman inside as she walked toward the end of
the building. Then she saw Chelsea getting out of the truck to
walk inside the office. From the way the truck was turned, she

wasn't able to get a better look at the driver before he drove out the front entrance.

She was tracking the truck's route when Cole pulled into the parking lot, surprising her by parking before he got out of the SUV to open the door for her.

"You didn't need to get out. I'm perfectly capable of opening my door."

"Why should you when I can?"

Making sure she was comfortable before closing the door, Cole got back in the car.

"Why were you waiting outside?" He fastened his seat belt and gave her a frowning glance. "I told you I would text when I was outside."

"I needed some fresh air," she told him, not wanting to share how hyper-aware she was of Chelsea listening to every sound she made through the shared wall. Though her freezing her butt off had been unnecessary, anyway, with Chelsea coming in late.

Snuggling into a warm, heated seat, Megan put Chelsea out of her mind.

"So, are you going to finally tell me where you're taking me to? I have to admit, when I said I would go out with you, I kinda imagined a dinner date, not a breakfast date. Not that I'm complaining," she hastened to assure him. "Breakfast is my favorite meal of the day."

"I told you to keep your whole day open," he reminded her.

Admiring how confidently he drove on the snowy road, she still started to get concerned as the weather was gradually getting worse. "The way it's snowing, perhaps we should just postpone this for another day." She really didn't want to spend the whole day isolated in her hotel room.

The only reason she hadn't found somewhere to live was that the need for a new car was greater. Without a reliable vehicle, she wouldn't be able to afford an apartment, so it was a catch twenty-two.

"Don't worry about the weather." A secretive smile played across his lips.

"Okay, but if we get stuck in Jamestown, it's going to be on you where to find a place to stay."

"We're not going to Jamestown."

Megan shot him a surprised glance. "Jamestown is the only place this road leads to, unless you take one of the back roads to Virginia, and it's snowing too heavily to drive through the mountains."

"We're not going to Virginia." Slowing the SUV, Cole put the blinker on.

"Oh ... I've never been on this road before." She did not recognize the sideroad cutting through a heavily wooded area of the mountain.

"You haven't?"

"Nope." The surrounding woods gave no clue of what lay ahead. Eager, she sat up straighter, wanting to see where they were going.

When he turned a corner, she gave him a questioning glance. "Treepoint has an airport?"

"Yes, only small airplanes can fly out of here."

"I guess that's why I didn't know we had an airport—I don't have my own plane," she joked.

"I don't, either." Parking the SUV next to a building, he turned toward her. "But I do have a friend who has offered me his pilot and plane for the day."

Her eyes widened. "You want to fly me somewhere?"

"I have a sightseeing boat. A friend of mine runs it for me while I'm on vacation. Another boat scraped the hull, and Ian wants me to settle the damages before the owner of the other boat flies back to Santa Barbara. I thought you could keep me company."

"I won't be in the way?"

"No, the meeting shouldn't take long. Then we can spend the rest of the day together. Are you game? I should have asked you, but if I asked you over the phone, I was afraid you would have told me no."

Megan arched a knowing brow in his direction. "You mean, it's easier to convince me when you're with me."

"That, too," he admitted.

"At least you're honest." She laughed, unfastening her seat belt.

"So, you'll go?"

"I should really put up more of a fight, but since my other choices are spending the rest of the day in my hotel room or watching Marty fry hamburgers, I don't want to chance you'll have a change of heart about taking me along."

A mixture of emotions played across Cole's face before he lifted her chin to lock their eyes together. "There's something I should have warned you about me. My heart isn't fickle. I'm steadfast and true. Once I love someone, I love them forever." Leaning toward her, he brushed a kiss on her cheek. It was such a tender gesture that it brought tears to her eyes.

"Ready?"

"Oh yes." Excited, she couldn't help but jump in her seat.

"There's that smile I was looking for ..." Cole grinned as he turned the engine off.

Megan couldn't help but smile as he got of the car to open the door for her. After closing the door, he gently raised the hood on her coat, hooked an arm over her shoulders, and attentively led her to the other side of the building.

Her jaw dropped when she saw the plane the building had hid from view. Giving him a searching glance, she managed to close her mouth. "I'm impressed." She was awestruck. She had never seen a real-life plane like this before except on television. "Cole, exactly who is your friend?"

"Have you heard of the band Mouth2Mouth?"

"Of course." She nodded. "I love their music."

"They use this plane to get to their concerts."

"That's so nice of them to lend it to you. You must be close friends."

"We are. When I asked to borrow the plane from Kaden, I told him there was something I needed to do."

"To meet the insurance agent." She nodded her head, still stunned she was about to get on a plane that Mouth2Mouth flew on.

Cole shook his head with a wide grin. "No, I told him I wanted to impress a girl."

Fifteen

"Would you like another drink?" the bartender offered.

"No, thank you. I haven't finished this one."

Sitting at the small drink stand at the marina where Cole had left her to wait for him, she checked her cell phone for the time. He should be back any minute. Tempted to pinch herself that she was at a marina in California and not still in a mental care facility, Megan decided she didn't want to know if this was a figment of her imagination.

Putting on the sun hat Cole had purchased for her from a clothing boutique when had arrived, she hopped off the stool and walked down the dock to where Cole was going to bring his boat back to moor.

As she raised her face to the sun, she couldn't understand why Cole would rather spend December in Treepoint than staying here, where it was sunny and warm. Not to mention the sun wasn't hiding behind layers and layers of clouds.

He had told her they needed to make a stop before meeting his friend and took her to the clothing boutique. Once they were there, he had her pick out an outfit for the day. At first, she had protested. Then she realized she wouldn't have to spend the day in a thick sweater and jeans and gave in.

Hastily placing a hand on her hat, she barely managed to keep it from flying away. When she heard a swooshing sound coming nearer, she looked around to see where it was coming from.

Hearing oo's and ahh's from people on their boats, Megan looked up at the sky at what they were staring at.

"What the heck ...?" Startled, her eyes widened to their fullest as Cole zoomed across the water with what looked like fire hoses attached to his feet. At the end of the dock, he slowly lowered himself until his feet were above the water, motioning to her.

Laughing, she ran over to him. "What are you doing?"

"It's called flyboarding." He laughed and held his hand out to her. "Come ride with me."

"I've never done it before! Is it hard?"

"All you have to do is hang on to me and not let go, no matter how scared you get. Can you do that?" Cole asked, holding both of his hands out to her.

Had she ever given anyone that much trust? No, she hadn't. She had married Curt knowing she would never trust anything he said or did.

Taking a deep breath, she reached out to take Cole's hands.

"Step onto the platform between my feet," he instructed her. "Wrap your arms around my neck."

Gingerly stepping onto the platform, she shyly wrapped her arms around Cole's neck.

"Hold on tighter."

Tightening her arms, she gasped as Cole slowly rose into the air. She expected the movements to be jerky and was amazed at how smoothly he was able to control the powerful jets as he glided back and forth over the water as if they were slowly dancing to music only they could hear.

The experience was exhilarating, exciting, frightening, and so amazingly beautiful she couldn't believe it was happening to her. This was an experience other women were meant to have, never her. She didn't deserve it.

"Megan!" Cole's sharp voice brought her back to awareness. "Whatever you're thinking, stop it right now! Have some fun!"

"Okay!"

Keeping his hands on her waist, Cole said something into his headset as he did a downward spiral until their feet dipped into the water.

"You better not get me wet!" she yelled out laughingly to him.

As he did a big loop, Megan heard music coming from the Jet Ski, which Cole's equipment was attached to, allowing them to be propelled into the air.

It took another series of loops and dips before she realized Cole was coordinating his movements with the song.

When he performed one graceful swirl, Megan closed her eyes, letting the music and Cole carry her away. She didn't open them when she felt Cole sweep her off her feet to carry her through the sky.

Who needed a hot air balloon when she had Cole?

Dreamily, she let go and just let him hold her, not wanting the ride to ever end as she listened to the haunting lyrics of "Shallow" by Lady Gaga.

She was at a loss for words when the ride ended, gazing wistfully at the Jet Ski as Cole removed first his helmet, then hers.

"We'll do it again another day," he promised, handing the helmets to the man on the Jet Ski.

She nodded, knowing it was unlikely. Cole would be

leaving after Christmas, and she would probably never see him again.

Numerous times, she had promised herself once she accomplished what she needed to in Treepoint, she would be free to move on with her life, knowing she was lying to herself. She would die in Treepoint just as generations before her had.

"Ready?"

Dragging herself out the gloomy thoughts of Cole leaving Treepoint, she gave him a bright smile. "Sure. Are we going back to the airport?"

"Not yet. I thought we could go sightseeing on my boat, unless you're anxious to get home?"

Home? She hadn't had a home since she had left her parents to marry Curt.

"No, I'd love to go on your boat. Which one is it?"

"This one." Cole nodded toward the boat next to them.

"You're kidding."

"Nope, this is mine," he stated proudly.

"Wow." The dark blue and white boat was sleek, nothing like what she had imagined it to look like. It was three times larger than expected, and its stunning beauty and sleek design stood out even with hundreds of boats in the marina.

"Uh, Cole ...?"

"Yes? Is there something wrong?"

Hastily shaking her head, she embarrassedly looked away from the two people waiting for them to board. "What if I get seasick? I've never been on a boat before."

"I got you covered. I have patches on board if you get sick. We'll come right back if you're not enjoying yourself. Okay?"

"Okay."

Her enthusiasm returned. No woman wanted to get an upset stomach on their first date.

All her insecurities made her doubt herself as Curt's voice played in the back of her mind like a broken recording, telling her that she would do something ignorant and humiliate herself. He had even given her a nickname, which had made her cringe every time he used it.

She'd had a wonderful day so far, and the more time spent with Cole, the more worried she became that she would likely do something that would gross him out. Then a new fear was unlocked of her having to hang over the side of the ship to puke her guts out while everyone watched.

When Cole helped her onto the boat, Megan stood, afraid to move. Never in a million years had she thought a girl like her would ever get the opportunity to be on a boat this size. She didn't deserve being here, and if she were a better person, she would ask Cole to take her back to Treepoint without taking another step. *You can be a better person tomorrow, Megan.*

Her guilty conscience dwindled. Even death row prisoners were given a last meal to enjoy.

Looking around at the magnificent ship then to the beautiful man who was looking at her in a way no one had looked at her before, she fought the tears that desperately wanted to fall.

This must be what it felt like to be in a fairy tale, but she was no Cinderella. Happily ever afters weren't meant for her; only exploding pumpkins.

"What is it?" he asked, sweetly wiping the tear that had finally escaped.

"I'm afraid of it turning midnight."

Sixteen

Megan sat on the bench seat next to Cole as the boat slowly rocked on the soft waves. Cole had dropped anchor as the sun had gone down.

He left her alone to head below deck, then came back to take her hand and lead her downstairs.

"I planned for us to eat a romantic dinner on deck, but the wind is working against me tonight."

Taking the seat Cole held out, she stared at the table appreciatively.

"I've never had a candlelit dinner before."

"I wish they were real."

"They're real to me." Placing the napkin on her lap, she almost held her arm out for Cole to pinch.

"What's so funny?"

"I was just thinking, if the cat we saved hadn't already been adopted, I would have adopted him when we got back."

Cole laughed with her as he filled her plate with salmon from a small, wooden plank, several fancy potatoes that looked too pretty to eat, and a roll.

"You're feeling guilty you didn't take him with you, aren't you?"

"Yes," she admitted. "I wanted to, but I've never had a pet, and I was afraid I would hurt it by mistake."

Cole dropped his fork onto his plate. "You don't really think that, do you?"

Embarrassed, she stared down at her plate. "My mother and father were allergic to animals, so they never let me have one. I wanted a puppy when I married Curt. He told me I could have a puppy when I showed him I could take care of our baby."

"That moth—"

Megan raised her eyes, finding Cole's jaw clenched, appearing as if he was biting back saying something.

"It's okay, Cole. In one way, Curt was right. I didn't know how to care for a baby. I had bought baby books and watched videos to prepare myself, but I had planned to ask for Mrs. James' help. She's the smartest woman I know."

As she talked, she noticed Cole was staring away from her. She cocked her head, listening.

"Are you worried about the wind? If we need to head back in, we can. If you don't think it's safe—"

Cole turned his face forward to start eating. "It's safe," he said gruffly. "If the wind picks up any more, Ian will radio me. Try the salmon. Let me know if you like it."

"I like it," she told him after taking a bite.

For the rest of the meal, Cole talked about how he had learned to flyboard after he left Queens City. "When Casey heard I took the instructor course, she flew down here and let me have it. I've never seen her so angry."

"What did you do?"

"I took her for a ride. She's still not happy about it, but she cuts me some slack during the holidays."

Megan licked her suddenly dry lips. "Is it dangerous?"

"I'm very careful." His gentle eyes soothed her worries. "I'm also very good."

She gave a relieved laugh. "I saw that."

"Did you enjoy it?"

"What do you think? It was amazing. You had quite a crowd watching, too. Do you usually give people rides?"

"All the time. Ian, my business partner, handles the sightseeing tours. I mainly do the flyboarding training and boat rentals."

Megan pushed her plate away, unable to eat more. "Rentals? You have more than one boat?"

Cole slid the dessert plate forward. "Try the cheesecake strawberries. I had Ian get them for me. They're my favorite."

She picked one up and took an experimental nibble to see if her stomach could handle more. After tasting it, she decided she would make room.

Giving her an approving look, he reached for his own plate. "I have four boats and six Jet Skis. This is my boat. I have a party boat to rent out, which Ian and I are co-owners of. I own a charter boat, which I rent for fishing. Also one that Kaden and I co-own together."

Megan shoved the last of the strawberries into her mouth to prevent herself from saying something stupid. What she knew about boats could be written on a Post-it note, and only then if she wrote in large print.

"Now you know why I wanted you to try the strawberries. They were good, weren't they?"

"Delicious," she mumbled, nearly choking getting the word out.

Carrying the plates to the sink, Cole glanced at the clock on the wall. He folded his arms over his chest and leaned back against the sink. "It's getting late."

Megan felt her heart sink. Midnight was coming sooner than she had expected.

"We have two choices, and I'm going to let you choose which one you want to do."

Megan took a sip of water. "Okay."

"We can fly back to Treepoint tonight, or we can spend the night here and fly back in the morning."

"Is it safe for you to sleep, or will you have to stay up?"

"I will be sleeping. That's why there's a captain on the top deck."

"Oh ... duh ..." Megan slapped her forehead. "I should—"

"Cut it out. You asked because you didn't want to have to stay awake all night instead of being able to sleep if we flew back. There was nothing stupid in your question."

"I forgot there were other people on board." Fiddling with her tiny earring, she tried to stem the rush of color she felt rushing to her cheeks.

"They're paid to be unobtrusive." His gentle smile eased the awkwardness she was feeling.

"Then I vote we stay the night here. I've never slept on a boat before."

"Then I second your vote. I'll make sure I have you back before the lunch rush."

She wondered about Marty. She was worried about the big lug.

"If you're worried about the money—"

Megan raised her hand, not wanting to hear whatever he was about to say. "I appreciate it, but I wasn't thinking about money. I was thinking about Marty. Something is wrong with his legs, and he refuses to go to the doctor."

Cole frowned. "I would have never known. Marty acts as if he's a heavyweight fighter just waiting for his next takedown."

"I thought so, too, until I went to the kitchen and saw how much pain he's in. I haven't been able to get him to see a doctor, no matter how hard I've tried."

Cole's frown disappeared. "I know his secret weakness."

"What's that?"

"Ginny. She's Matthew and Issac's little sister."

Megan nodded. "I know her. How is she Marty's weakness?"

"They are close, but he would deny it to hell and back."

"Then how do you—"

"Ginny toured with Mouth2Mouth."

She knew that, also. Everyone in Treepoint was aware of how famous Ginny had become before getting married and returning to Treepoint, leaving her singing career behind.

"That's how she met Marty. When a tornado hit the restaurant Marty owned in Tennessee, he didn't rebuild there; he bought the diner in Treepoint instead."

"You think she'd talk to him?"

"For sure. I'll call her in the morning."

"Thank you. That'll be a big burden off my mind."

"Glad to help." Straightening off the sink, he went to the table and turned the candles off.

Despondently, she felt as if the joy had been sucked out of the room.

"Let me show you where you'll be sleeping."

She trailed after Cole as they went through a narrow hallway to the end, coming to a halt next to three doors. His shoulder brushed against hers as he opened the door behind her.

"This is your room." Raising his hand, he tapped on the door next to hers with his knuckles. "This is the bathroom. I keep extra robes and pajamas there. Help yourself to anything you need."

"You bring a lot of guests?"

Did you really think you were the only woman Cole has treated to a date on his boat? You're such a nitwit. There's nothing special about you.

"I loan the boat to several people." Cole shrugged. "Sometimes, they plan ahead. Others, they do it spur of the moment."

"Ah ... that makes sense."

Cole didn't directly say he hadn't had a date aboard before, but neither did he say he had. She was good with that. She'd rather not know.

"Can I get you anything?"

"No." Megan cleared her throat nervously. "Where will you be sleeping?"

Cole nodded his head back. "This is my room. Just knock or text me."

"All right ... good night."

"Night."

Inside, Megan closed the door. The light was already on, and the bed turned down. She walked toward the bed and ran her hand over the silky-soft sheets. Sitting down on the side, she looked at the closed door instead of throwing herself down on the luxurious bed, as her younger self would have done. She didn't care about the monetary things Cole possessed, nor the promises she had made herself not to become involved with him or any man until she was surer of her mental health. What did bother her was that she was alone.

She was so tired of being alone. Of being scared to the root of her being she would die that way. No one to mourn her loss, no one to cry over her grave, no one who would even bother to put a headstone up. No one to remember that she had ever existed.

Cole made her feel as if she actually did exist. Her greatest fear was that she would die in her sleep, and her body wouldn't be discovered until the housecleaner came to clean her room at the motel.

Not wanting to sleep anymore, Megan decided to take a shower.

She went to the bathroom, showered, and washed her hair. Searching the drawers, she found a hair dryer and an unopened hairbrush.

She stared at herself in the mirror as she blew her hair out and came to a conclusion. There was a way she could keep her promise to herself and not have to be alone tonight. There was only one hiccup in her plan.

Cole.

Seventeen

 ❦

M egan bit her bottom lip as she raised her hand to knock on Cole's door.

You're going to make a fool of yourself.

It won't be the first time, she argued back to herself.

I'm just going to ask him to let me sleep with him, she lied to herself.

Pfft. You want to jump his bones.

Caught in the lie, Megan used the other excuse she had on standby.

It will be only for one night, and it'll be just for sex. I won't get emotionally involved.

Her conscience stayed eerily silent.

You'll see, I won't fall in love with him, she assured her conscience, knocking on the door before she could change her mind.

You already are.

You would have been more helpful if you had said that before I freaking knocked.

Lord, have mercy. Her tongue went to the roof of her

mouth when Cole answered the door only wearing pajama bottoms.

He looked at her in concern. "Is something wrong?"

Her mind went completely blank staring at him.

"Uh ... I ..."

Cole stood patiently.

She was acting so weird that she was surprised he hadn't slammed the door in her face.

"Take a deep breath."

Drawing a deep breath into her lungs, she released it then wished she had brushed her teeth.

"Never mind. I'm sorry I disturbed you."

Cole caught her by the arm, preventing her from running back to her room. "Megan, what did you want?"

His patience had her able to loosen her tongue. Licking her bottom lip, she played with the belt tied at her waist. "I don't want to be alone," she told him, staring down at the floor.

"Do you mean right now or all night?"

"All night."

At his silence, Megan dared to look through her lashes to find him staring at her in amusement.

"I just want to be clear. A guy can't be too careful ... Do you want a friendly sleepover, or are you suggesting something more *intimate*?"

Megan ground her teeth. Why did he want her to say it out loud?

Pulling the belt tighter, she tried to think of what a more experienced woman would say.

"Megan, if you tighten that belt any tighter, you're not going to be able to breathe."

She pushed her hands into her pockets and lifted her eyes. "I wouldn't be opposed to sex."

Cole gathered both dangling ends of her robe in his hands,

twining them around and drawing her closer to his body. "I wouldn't be opposed to having sex with you either."

Megan licked her lip again. "You wouldn't?"

"Nope." Seductively, the hand holding the belt brushed against her breast as he pulled her even closer. "I just want to make one thing clear before we do this."

Megan frowned. "What?"

"I don't have sex with just anyone."

"I don't, either."

"Then we're in agreement." Cole stepped back into the room, tugging her forward with him.

Confused, Megan felt as if she was being lured into a trap. "What did we agree on?"

"That you're mine." Cole dropped the tie of the robe to close the door and lean against it.

She shook her head. "I didn't agree to that."

"You did."

"I think I would remember saying that. I didn't." Nervously, she started backing up when Cole used his back to push away from the door and started walking toward her. Coming to a stop when she felt the bed behind her knees, she rested a hand to his chest. That might have been the wrong thing to do—feeling his smooth skin under her palm.

"I don't let anyone invite themselves into my bed. What kind of guy do you think I am?"

"Uh ..." Megan delved deeper into his eyes then playfully tapped his chest. "You're just playing with me."

"Megan ..." The amusement in his eyes was replaced with something she couldn't decipher. "I haven't begun to play." When he took a step forward, Megan instinctively took another step back, forgetting the bed was behind her.

Falling backward, she gave a gasp as Cole placed a knee on the bed and leaned over her. Closing her eyes tightly, she clenched her hands in the blanket on the bed.

"Do you mind scooting up so I can lie down, too?"

Her lashes flew up. "Oh ... I'm sorry." Rolling over to get on her knees, she crawled to the head of the bed then wiggled to the side to make more room for Cole.

"You mind if I turn the lights off?"

"Not at all."

Soft moonlight filtered through the curtains when Cole turned the lights off.

"Let's grab a nap. We have all night."

Didn't he want her?

Finding herself tucked into his side, Megan gazed up at the dark ceiling. Should she make the first move? They had left Treepoint early this morning, so he was probably tired.

Relaxing, she snuggled against his side, her hand going to his bare chest. His arm around her waist pulled her closer, and he left it there as they lay together.

The anxiety brought about by actually having sex with Cole gradually dissipated. Having sex had never been pleasurable with Curt, and the dread of finding out sex with Cole would be just as miserable made her regret knocking on his door.

Lying next to him brought back the heightened awareness, which had fled the moment he showed his desire for her. She was comfortable with the easy-going Cole who wouldn't hurt a kitten and was ceaselessly kind to her, which had given her the courage to knock on his door in the first place. Yet, the moment his features had hardened, displaying a different side of him when he bent to get on the bed with her, showed an overt masculinity that terrified her.

Having sex with Curt had been miserable and disgusting, so much so that she had developed several excuses to avoid the intimacy whenever possible. When she couldn't, he would make her pay the price until she found it easier to give in to his demands rather deal with the vile way he treated her.

When she was unable to resist rubbing her hand over Cole's chest, a revelation came to her. Cole was nothing like Curt. Curt would have run over the cat. That one little revelation had her nuzzling Cole's neck.

"I'm not sleepy," she whispered.

He rolled over until they were facing each other. "I'm not either," he whispered back.

Sliding her lips from Cole's neck to his mouth, she lightly rubbed them across the sensual curve of his. "I don't want to go to sleep," she murmured.

"Me, neither."

"Then why did you say you did?"

"I could tell you were afraid."

"I'm not anymore."

"I'm getting that message."

Megan could hear the amusement in his voice.

"Are you laughing at me?" she asked him suspiciously, raising her lips from his.

"No." Cole bent the arm under her neck to curl upward, tangling his fingers in her hair. "I want you too much to laugh at you. I'm laughing at myself." Using his shoulder, he pushed her onto her back to lean over her in the dark.

"Why?"

"You weren't the only one afraid."

Shocked at his answer, she wrapped her arms around his neck. The thought of Cole being afraid of anything brought out her protective instincts.

"Why were you afraid?" She went taut under him, ready to do battle.

"I was afraid I would break and not be the man you need me to be," he confessed.

She melted back into the mattress. "You're exactly the man I need."

Cole's lips hovered over hers, and he teasingly stroked his

tongue over her bottom lip. When she raised her head to deepen the kiss, Cole let his lips slide away. Back and forth, they played the sensual game until, growing frustrated, she buried her hand in his hair to keep him still.

As if she had lit a fuse, Cole's mouth hardened over hers, driving her head back onto the pillow. Taking command, he parted her lips, plunging his tongue inside then retreating, playing the same nerve-racking game, which made her want to scream.

Deciding to fight fire with fire, she unwound her arms and moved them to his waist. Tantalizingly, she ran her fingertips under the band of his pajama bottoms, then moved them higher, then brought them lower than before.

The game ended when she reached his hip and the back of her fingers accidentally found more than she had bargained for. Before her fingers could skitter away, though, Cole's hips jerked reflexively, bringing his cock in direct contact.

A low groan escaped him, sending a surge of power through her. The new feeling of being in control instead of being the recipient was mind blowing to her. Closing her hand over Cole's cock because she wanted to, not because she had to, let her appreciate the silky smooth flesh, the warmth.

Her fingers experimentally climbed higher to the tip, where she rubbed the pad of her thumb over the tip. Cole sucked in a hiss of air.

"I like touching you."

"You don't know how much I like you touching me," he groaned. "You can touch me all you want."

"I won't shock you?" Using her shoulder, she pushed until he was the one on his back. She leaned down and rubbed her mouth over his nipple.

"I'm unshockable."

Megan let her tongue play with the spiking nipple. "Should I try to prove you wrong?"

"God ... please ... prove me wrong."

She blew on the wet nipple at the same time her hand started gliding over his cock in firm strokes. Having Cole under her control was addicting. The more he responded, the naughtier she wanted to be.

Releasing his cock, she sat up to hop off the bed.

Cole rose onto his elbows and stared at her balefully. "You running out of the room is not how I want you to prove me wrong."

Megan giggled. then her hands went to his ankles, to the hem of his pajamas. "I wasn't leaving." Slowly, she started tugging the pajamas down until he was completely uncovered. The garment fell from her hand onto the floor.

"You're beautiful," she breathed.

Cole's body, highlighted by the soft light of the moon, was imprinted on her mind. If she had thought his face was beautiful, his body was a priceless piece of art.

"I wish I knew how to paint," she murmured. "How can one human be so beautiful?"

Cole's eyes met hers as he scooted down the bed to sit at the end, taking her face between his hands. "Because it's not how I look; it's how you see me."

Megan frowned. "I don't understand."

"I know you don't," he said softly. "But I promise you, you will." His hand went behind her neck to pull her down for a passionate kiss.

Becoming so enthralled with the sensations he was creating, she didn't notice him unbuttoning her satin top and sliding it off her shoulders, nor removing her bottoms. Their eyes clung together as Cole lifted her over him. Holding on to his shoulders, she bit her lip, expecting pain yet finding only pleasure so sweet she wanted to cry.

Straddling him, she slowly moved as his mouth explored every curve of her breasts. When his warm mouth covered a beaded nipple, she moved faster, but Cole wrapped his arms around her hips to slow her movements.

"Go faster," he urged. Over and over, he changed the speed of the game they were playing.

"I can't take it anymore. I need to come," she pleaded.

"You can when you tell me what I want to hear."

Her mind went blank. What in the hell was Cole waiting for her to say?

Her body was ready to riot when it suddenly clicked what he was waiting for.

"I'm yours."

Explosions went off in her body with a magnitude that she feared she would pass out. Cole must have sensed she had momentarily left her body as he curled his arms under her shoulders to hold her to his chest.

Resting her head on his shoulder, she sucked air into her oxygen-deprived lungs. "You're lethal."

Megan felt the curve of his smile against her neck.

"Nope." He mimicked her accent. "I'm yours."

Eighteen

Cole gently picked up a wayward curl laying on Megan's cheek as she slept next to him. Swallowing the lump in his throat, he knew the love he felt for this fragile woman grew stronger each day. So did the fear he felt for her. Some part of her past was eating her alive, and it showed in her appearance and the deep sorrow in her indigo-blue eyes.

Viper had warned him how delicate Megan's health was when he asked him to watch out for her after he came back from dropping the stray cat off at the shelter. Casey and Max were staying with Shade and Lily. Cole had noticed how Shade stopped talking to Max when Cole was telling Casey about the cat and meeting a girl named Megan. Shade then left and returned with Viper, asking him to come outside to talk.

Cole would never forget standing on the porch as Viper told him about Megan, the fucked-up way her dead husband had treated her, and that she had a psychotic break after losing her baby.

"Is this your roundabout way of telling me I should stay away from Megan?" he asked, already determined to find her.

"No, this my way of asking you to watch out for her. The kid never stood a chance against Curt. Her parents cared more about their reputation than doing what's right for their daughter. Since you're new in town, she might find it easier to confide in you if she needs any help."

"That's all you need me to do?" Cole rubbed the tip of his boot on the porch's floorboard. "Because if you want me to play spy for you, that isn't going to work for me."

"I don't need you to play spy for me." The President of The Last Riders gave him a formidable glance. "I have trained men capable of doing a much better job than you. All I need you to do is be a friend to her."

"What if it turns into more than friendship?"

Viper gave him a penetrating stare. "If a brother, or anyone else, said that to me, I'd tell them to hold off. The kid needs time to get her feet under her. From what her counselor told Diamond, Megan needs to prove to herself that she's mentally stronger and can make better choices than when she lived here before. The last thing she needs is to get involved with someone who could destroy what headway she's made. Where you're concerned, the worst thing you're capable of being is too kind. It gets fucking irritating. So, you know. Makes the rest of us look bad."

"And you just want me to help her?" Still. Cole did not quite believe Viper's goal was completely altruistic.

"No. that would defeat the purpose." Viper shook his head. "I just don't want her to fall. Megan kept a roof over Curt and her head while she was pregnant, and the son of a bitch kept making her switch jobs every fucking time anyone tried to help her. Megan is a fighter; she just doesn't believe in herself enough to realize that." Viper strode to the porch rail, giving him his back.

"I don't hold any ill will against Megan. I would have told her that today, but I could tell from the way she looked .."

Viper's voice turned gruff. "To be honest. I was so fucking shocked by the way she looked. If Curt wasn't already dead, I would have killed him with my bare hands. The rest of the brothers felt the same way. It wasn't easy to talk to her when all you want to do is dig up the bastard just to have the pleasure of grinding his bones to dust."

It had taken Viper several seconds before the rage left his face, turning to sorrow. "In some ways, she reminds me of Reaper. I learned from him that you have to let them get to the place where they're willing to listen. Megan isn't there yet. All I want you to do is fill that gap until she's ready to trust enough to let us in."

Viper had kept to his word and hadn't asked any questions about Megan.

Cole traced the outline of the delicate shell of her ear. Her skin was so translucent that you could see the tiny veins running underneath. Scooting closer to her rather than chance moving her, he tightened his arm around her waist.

God, how much he loved this woman. He no longer regretted the time he lain spent in a coma, nor the years he had spent more child than man. He was meant to be here, at this moment in time, for her. He thought it was so ironic she was worried about Marty when she was letting herself slip away without a fight.

Viper was right about one thing—she was fighter. The problem was she had been knocked down so many times she'd had the fight knocked out of her.

Today gave him hope. He had seen the flare of jealousy when she asked about the robes and pajamas. She had also shocked him when she knocked on his door.

Cole had to constantly watch his reactions not to scare her off. Megan was timid as a doe once she lowered her guard with him. He could practically read her mind. She had come prepared to have sex with him, then she would keep him at a distance as if it never happened. That was why he made certain she got his message—he was no one's one-night stand. Megan wasn't going to find it easy to return to Treepoint and resume their causal relationship. She was his, and he was going to make certain he didn't leave Treepoint without her, even if he had to stay there to convince her. All he had to do was careful. Her past was a minefield he had to navigate carefully, or he would damage her budding love for him.

When she had closed her eyes, he had been about to get out of the bed and throw cold water on the desire he was hiding from her. Thankfully, she had fought through what was holding her back and showed him the woman she could be when she wasn't afraid.

All his little fighter needed was confidence. The confidence to be herself, to know that someone was capable of loving her like she deserved to be loved and, most importantly, have the confidence to face the past. Cole feared that most of all. He was afraid if she lost that battle, there wouldn't be a way to get her back.

He ran a gentle hand over her short, curly hair and brushed his lips over her forehead.

"Why are you awake?" she murmured in a groggy voice.

"I wasn't finished loving you."

Megan buried her face in the covers. "I'm sleeping."

Cole grinned, rolling her onto her back. Then, pulling the cover down, he stared into wide-awake eyes. "What are *you* doing awake?"

Her body melted into his, her thighs going around his hips. "I guess I wasn't done loving you either."

Nineteen

Megan practically skipped after leaving Dustin's office. If she were any happier, her hot air balloon would be entering outer space.

Turning her heat on full blast once she was back in her car, she checked her gas gage, ecstatic she wouldn't have to swing by the gas station to complete the next delivery.

When she pulled out onto the road. she calculated how much more money she needed to buy Joel's car—a couple more days. And if the tips kept coming in the way they had been, she would have enough to buy Cole a nice Christmas present.

She was so worried about running out of time with having so much to get accomplished in the few days left before Christmas that she hadn't even bothered to look for an apartment. Right now, an apartment was the last of her priorities. *Car first, then an apartment*, she had to remind herself constantly.

Chelsea made living at the hotel unbearable. She constantly found something to badger her about, even when she had no cause. If there were another hotel in town, she would have left. Unfortunately, the next closest was in Jamestown, and her car wouldn't make the drive twice daily, especially in the icy weather they had been experiencing.

In her mind, she went over what she wanted to say as she passed The Last Riders' compound. Sparing it a brief glance, she spotted Cole's SUV.

She had seen him every day since they came back from California. She let him stay the first night back, but the next day, Chelsea had called her to the office.

From the moment she had walked inside the office, she knew Chelsea was going to pull something to get her to leave. And Chelsea didn't disappoint.

"You're not allowed overnight guests." she'd spat out. "You paid for a single. Cole stayed last night, so you owe twenty-five dollars, which needs to be paid immediately."

Paying the twenty-five had hurt, as she was on a tight budget.

"If I catch you trying to sneak anyone else in, you'll be asked to leave immediately."

Embarrassed that Chelsea was talking so nastily in front of the day clerk, she almost slunk out of the office in shame. Megan couldn't explain what the turning point was when she took her last BS from Chelsea.

She gave Chelsea the cold shoulder and walked to stand in front of Harford. "Can you give me the name and number of the owner?"

Chelsea shoved Harford aside. "Why do you want his number?"

"I wasn't talking to you, Chelsea," she said coldly. Returning her attention back to Harford, she continued talking as if Chelsea weren't listening. "I have done nothing to deserve the way Chelsea speaks to me. I plan to make him aware of the treatment I have been receiving, and if I am asked to leave without a valid reason after I have paid for the room in advance, I will seek legal advice." Megan held out her hand to Harford. "I'd like the owner's number."

"I'm the manager," Chelsea blustered. "Zack won't care about your complaints."

"Maybe not, but I'm still going to call."

Taking the card from Harford's hand, Megan noticed the hateful way Chelsea was looking at her. A cold shiver ran down her back. It was filled with such spitefulness that it stopped her from leaving. Chelsea knew she had frightened her.

"I would think twice, sloth brains," she jeered.

Megan felt the color drain of out her cheeks. She would rather Chelsea had struck her than use the nickname Curt had constantly tormented her with during their marriage.

Giving Chelsea her back, she took a step forward, then another, until she found herself out of the office. She immediately went to her car. Megan refused to give Chelsea the pleasure of listening to her cry in her room. She'd waited until she parked beside the dumpster of the diner to break into tears.

Why did Chelsea hate her so much? She had tried to be friends with her, but Chelsea would laugh with her friends about every little thing about her, from the type of clothes she wore, her hair, and she had even been told Chelsea made fun of the way she wore her makeup until it was easier not to wear any.

When she reached the Coleman's driveway, Megan turned on her blinker. She needed to put the confrontation with Chelsea to the back of her mind. She had held off calling her manager, hoping the threat alone would be sufficient. She might dislike Chelsea, but she also didn't want to take a chance to ger her fired right before Christmas.

"You've got this." Parking her car, Megan nervously walked to Silas' front door, where she took a deep breath before she knocked.

Silas came to the door, raising his brow at her. "Hi, Megan. Which of the boys ordered lunch? They could have at least waited until the stew was done."

Megan shook her head. "I'm not here for a delivery. If you have a few minutes, I have something I'd like to talk to you about. That is, if you're not busy." Megan started backing up at seeing Ginny walk up behind Silas. "I can come back later?"

"Megan, at least let me answer before you take off." Silas laughed. "We're just sitting around, writing a grocery list of what we need from the store for Christmas dinner. If you want a private conversation, I can get my jacket."

"No, that won't be necessary. The favor I want to ask involves your family. I was going to ask you first and get your opinion, but I might as well get it over with."

"Might as well." He smiled.

Megan wanted to take a nose-dive off the front porch. "I didn't mean it to come out that way. When I get nervous, my mouth works faster than my brain," she apologized.

Silas stepped back. motioning her to come inside. "We must be related," he teased. "My big-mouthed brothers have the same problem."

Stepping inside, she shook her head when Ginny offered to take her coat. "No, thank you. I don't want to take up much of your time." Licking her dry lips under the scrutiny of Silas and his sister, she timorously followed Silas into the huge living room.

"Have a seat," Silas offered.

"I prefer to stretch my legs out. I spend too much time in my car."

Silas nodded in understanding, and Megan just stood there, unable to talk with everyone staring at her.

"You have a favor to ask?" Silas prompted.

"Could I buy a plot in your family cemetery?"

❄

Megan tapped her cold feet on the driver's mat as she waited outside the church. She would give it a couple more minutes before she left. If the pastor didn't arrive, she would have to come back later.

She was about to put the car in *Reverse* when she saw the pastor pull into the parking lot.

She got out of her car while the pastor parked but remained standing in her spot, deliberately putting herself in the pastor's eyesight, giving him the opportunity to enter the church through a different entrance.

He walked in her direction, coming to a stop in front of her. "Good afternoon, Megan. Chilly day, isn't it?"

"Good afternoon, Pastor. Do you have a few minutes to spare? I would like to talk with you, if you have the time?" she asked uncertainly.

"You're in luck. I have some free time."

Megan gave the pastor a tentative smile, appreciating his play of words.

"Come inside. My office is much warmer. I'll have Willa make us some cocoa."

"This shouldn't take long." Embarrassed, she looked away. The pastor's wife had the patience of a saint. Which, admittedly, Megan had tried frequently as a teen, yet Willa had remained unfailingly kind to her. Her guilt on how she had done Willa wrong when she quit without notice still bothered her so bad the sight of a cupcake would make her nauseous. "I'm sure Willa is busy getting ready for the church's Christmas dinner."

"She'd make time for you," he assured her. "But I understand if you're busy with your delivery job. What can I do for you?"

"I know I'm not a member of this church, so I'm willing to pay, but ... would you give a sermon at a funeral for me?"

Cole was waiting for her when she arrived back at the hotel.

Approaching him, she gave him a mock scowl. "I told you I couldn't see you tonight."

"You said you *might not* be able to see me tonight," he corrected her. "You were supposed to call me ten minutes ago. When you didn't, I took that as a yes."

Megan rolled her eyes at him. "Most men would take that as a no."

"I'm not most men," Cole bragged, then tried to look pitiful. "If I were, I would have died."

Giving him a narrowed-eyed stare, she opened the door to let him inside. "You can't stay long, or Chelsea will be over here, demanding another twenty-five dollars."

She had told Cole about Chelsea making her pay for him spending the night. He had wanted to talk to the owner himself. It had taken her over an hour to convince him to let her take care of the situation. Since then, Cole would stay only a few hours. Often, they would just walk about Treepoint while admiring the Christmas lights.

"She won't come while I'm here."

"You don't know that."

"Then let's bet. I'll stay the night and see if she comes over."

Megan folded her arms over her chest. "She told me if you stay the night again, she'll throw me out."

"About that; I found you a place for rent which fits into your budget. It's—"

Megan pressed her fingers over Cole's lips. "Car first, then apartment," she repeated the same refran to Cole which she told herself constantly. "After I pay off the car tomorrow and get the tags, you can tell me about the apartment."

He mumbled through her finger, "It's not an apar—"

"Cole ..." She glared at him warningly.

His shoulders slumped. "You win."

Megan removed her fingers. "You want to watch a show?"

"Can I pick the show?" he bargained.

Megan started taking off her coat. "As long as it's not *Ninety-Day Fiancé*."

Cole looked crushed at her for nixing his favorite program. "You don't believe in falling in love and getting married in ninety days?"

"Those couples need Jesus more than they need marriage."

They took off their shoes and climbed onto the bed. After turning the television on, Megan laid her head on Cole's shoulder as they started watching *Single and Searching*.

"Are you going to let me stay the night?"

Megan linked her fingers with his. "Probably."

"How can I get you to change your answer from *probably* to a yes?" He pulled her tighter to him.

"I could be persuaded if we watch *Miracle on 34ᵗʰ Street*."

"We can do that."

Switching the channel, she got up to turn the lights off before settling back next to Cole.

"You're very quiet tonight. Is something wrong? I can leave if you're worried about Chelsea."

Megan raised her head to meet his eyes. "Is it okay if I fall in love with you?"

Bemusement filled Cole's eyes. "You're asking me permission to fall in love with me?"

"Yes. There's no need for me to fall if you tell me no from the get-go."

Cole slid down on the bed then tugged her over him. "You have my permission. Fall away."

"Aren't you going to ask me?" Megan propped her head on his chest as she waited for his answer.

"No."

"Why not?"

"Because I fell in love with you at the get-go."

Twenty

M egan took the coward's way out by leaving with Cole in the morning. She wasn't proud of herself for using Cole as a shield, but the only alternative was another confrontation with Chelsea. Cole, on the other hand, wanted her to let him have a talk with her.

"We've been at each other's throats since we were in middle school. The best way to handle her is to ignore her."

Cole's brows pulled together. "I don't think so. You two are adults, or at least one of you is. Ignoring her isn't working. I don't feel good about you staying here. I wish—"

"Cole ..."

"Okay ... But if she gets out of line one more time, I'm going to step in, Megan, whether you like it or not."

Her hands went to her hips. "I don't need you to fight my battles for me."

"I don't plan to fight the battle for you. I plan to end it."

Megan walked away from him in a huff.

"I'll call you later!" he yelled after her.

She was glad her back was to him so he couldn't see the smile on her face.

Why did he have to be so irresistible?

Her first stop was the gas station, where she paid Joel for his car. She felt such a surge of accomplishment when he handed her the bill of sale that she hugged him.

"I appreciate you not selling the car until I had the money."

"No problem." Red-faced, Joel gave her the keys. "What are you going to do with your old car?"

Megan shrugged. "I haven't really thought about it. Any ideas?"

"I could take it off your hands for the right price. I can work on it in my spare time."

"That would be great."

They came to an agreement on the price, and Megan was ecstatic. The money would give her a head start on a deposit for an apartment and buy a present for Cole.

"Do you have the title for the car?" Joel asked.

"I have it back at my hotel room. I'll swing by before I go the courthouse to register my new one."

"All right. I'll see you then."

She emptied what was left in her old car and transferred the contents to the new one.

When she drove out of the gas station and back to the hotel, she noticed Chelsea's boyfriend's truck was parked outside the office. It gave her pause. Harford had told her he was working today. She drove around the building to the side her room was on and turned the engine off. After taking the hotel card out of her purse, Megan got out of the car, her mind on getting to the courthouse before orders started coming in.

When she opened the door, Megan jumped at seeing Chelsea standing in front of the bed.

"What are ...?" Her eyes went to Chelsea's hand. She was holding a thick stack of papers as if on a mission.

Looking toward the bed, Megan saw pictures spread out on top.

She left the door open as she walked toward the photos, where she bent down and picked one up.

Sick to her stomach, Megan sat down on the end of the bed.

Her sitting down infuriated Chelsea, who, recovering from her surprise at getting caught, flung the rest of the photographs at her face. "I want you out of here!"

Megan didn't flinch, numbly sitting there. "I'm getting that message."

"If you don't leave, I'm going to make certain your boyfriend gets these pictures. He won't think you're such hot shit when he sees these."

Unable to bear the venom coming from Chelsea, she lowered her eyes to the photograph she was holding. The graphic picture made her stomach recoil.

"Why?" She lifted her gaze back to Chelsea. "Why does it matter to you so much? I don't ..." Oh my god. The reason for Chelsea's animosity had been right there the whole time.

Megan closed her eyes in anguish, pressing her fingers to her forehead. "I wasn't the only one Curt was blackmailing, was I?" Opening her eyes, she caught the frightened expression before Chelsea could mask it.

"You think I'd pose for pictures like these?" Chelsea gave her a disgusted look. "I'm not the one with sloth brains ..."

Megan gave her a pitying look. "I should have caught it when you used the nickname Curt gave me." Megan gave bitter laugh, wadding the paper in her hand. "Curt swore to me that I was the only one he was involved with in school." Megan raised a hand to fan herself to keep from crying. The last thing she wanted was to cry in front of Chelsea.

"I wasn't involved with Curt," Chelsea insisted stubbornly. "He—"

"You don't have to lie to me. God knows I know what a manipulative bastard he was. Who did he pretend to be when he started texting you? I thought he was Robbie." Megan gave the name of their classmate who was so popular at school she couldn't believe he was texting her. "I fell for it hook, line, and sinker, right up to the point I let him convince me to take a picture of my boobs when I knew better, but we both know how convincing Curt could be, don't we?"

Chelsea turned her gaze away from her.

"I even let him convince me to meet him after school, thinking it was Robbie. I met him at the library. I told my mom I was trying to bring my test score up. She was so proud of me. When Curt showed instead, I was so scared I thought I would vomit. I told him I was going to tell my parents, and he threatened me that if I did, he would make sure everyone in Treepoint saw that boob picture. I was so scared when he made me leave with him. I didn't want to go with him, but I didn't want my parents to know how stupid I was to take that picture after all their warnings. He drove me out to one of the back roads, pulled over, and—"

"I don't want to hear—" Chelsea interrupted.

"—raped me," Megan continued as if Chelsea hadn't interrupted. "I was fourteen years old. How old were you?"

When Chelsea remained silent, Megan reasoned her answer wouldn't be forthcoming.

"After that time, he made me meet him every Saturday." Megan picked up another picture from the bed. "Curt did love taking pictures, didn't he? When he wanted me to marry him, I tried to kill myself. The thought of having sex with him anytime he wanted it was more than I could handle." Megan gave Chelsea a wry smile. "But not enough to go through with it. Like everything else, I chickened out and married him. I humiliated my parents badly enough they left town when I married Curt. The only thing that made my life bearable was that at least my parents never found out about these pictures."

"They will if you don't leave. So will the whole town," Chelsea threatened.

"I'll leave." Megan rose stiffly from the bed and moved to the closet to take out her suitcase. Setting it on the mattress, she opened it, then went to the dresser to remove her clothes.

Satisfied she was leaving, Chelsea went to the door. "I'll have your checkout papers waiting. Don't be long."

"Curt might have been a terrible person, but he was a good coach. He covered his bases, didn't he, Chelsea?" Megan carried her clothes to the suitcase, staring at Chelsea in the doorway. "I never gossiped about you or made fun of you. He made sure we hated each other enough to stay away from one another. I'd say so we couldn't compare notes.

"He always used a different phone when he took pictures of me. I would try to find it when he was sleeping so I could destroy it. I take it you had it. I'm also assuming you think I have the cell phone containing your pictures?"

The fear on Chelsea's face was heart-wrenching. Any hatred she felt toward her died. Chelsea was just another victim, like she had been.

"Sorry, I don't. If I did, I would have destroyed it."

"I don't believe you. Evan is going to ask me to marry him Christmas Eve. If you post any of my pictures, I'll—"

"Is that why you tried to kill me with his truck?"

"If I wanted you dead, you'd be dead. I should have known you were too stupid to take the warning. Let's see if you can get this through your brain. Get out of Treepoint!" Chelsea screeched at her. "We're both better off with you gone."

There was no reasoning with her. Megan could understand her fear.

"I'm leaving the hotel, but I'm not leaving Treepoint until I bury my daughter tomorrow."

Chelsea gave her a curt nod. "I'd take those pictures with you," she said snidely. "The cleaner has a habit of being nosy."

Megan gave the woman a look of pity. "Curt is dead, and he still has us at each other's throat. He's still winning."

Chelsea sneered at her. "Don't act all high and mighty. You don't want that good-looking boyfriend seeing those pictures any more than I want Evan seeing mine."

"The sad thing is I now know who has my pictures; you don't know who has yours," Megan warned her. "Or if they have both of ours."

"I'll take my chances, but with you gone, I'll have one thing less to consider," she said cryptically.

She slammed the door after her, and Megan sighed. Chelsea made it hard to like her.

After packing the rest of her clothes, she gathered all the pictures and shoved them into the suitcase. She checked to make sure she hadn't left anything behind, then put the suitcase into her car before driving around to the front.

Strangely, she wasn't afraid to go inside the office. She was still too numb to feel much of anything.

When she reached the counter, Chelsea pushed the copy of the bill toward her with seventy-eight dollars sitting on top.

"Here you go. This is your refund for the three days you paid in advance."

Megan took the money and bill and put them in her purse.

"Bye, Harford. You both have a Merry Christmas."

Chelsea gave her insincere smile. "You, too."

Harford didn't respond, giving her a concerned look. Megan sent him a reassuring glance as she walked out the door.

Once she left the office, she stood and stared at the main

road, the businesses, the Christmas lights, taking it all in, committing each tiny detail to memory. When she left Treepoint this time, she was never coming back. She had lost too many parts of her heart to this town, and she wasn't going to give it one more piece.

Twenty-One

Megan was treated to Marty's glower when she walked into the diner.

"Where have you fucking been?"

"I sold my car and transfer—"

"Never mind. I don't give a fuck. Why aren't you taking orders? Fuckers coming here in person to place their orders."

"Sorry ... if it helps, I'm taking orders now."

"Don't do me any favors," he groused, his beady eyes turning to pinpoints. "Who in the hell shit on your parade?"

"I don't know what you mean." Taking a seat at the counter, Megan placed her delivery bag down next to her.

"Sure you don't," he said sarcastically. "I don't give a fuck, anyway. I have a bone to pick with you. Ginny came moseying her ass in here. When I need you sticking your nose into my business, I'll ask. Got it?"

"Pfft. How can I not—you're yelling." Megan arched her brows at him then grinned. "When's your appointment?"

"This afternoon, so no taking orders after three."

Marty hobbled back to the kitchen, leaving her sitting

alone at the counter. She was still waiting for an order when he came back to plop a bag in front of her.

"Since you want to stick your nose into my fucking business, I'm going to stick mine in yours. Fucking eat, or I'm going to shove it down your throat."

"I'll eat."

Megan didn't like the way he was looking at her. She opened the bag and started eating. She had finished and was throwing the bag away when orders came in. She spent the rest of the day fulfilling them. Right before Marty was going to close, she returned to the diner.

"What are you doing back? I told you I was closing for the rest of the day."

"I just wanted to stop by and wish you a Merry Christmas. I won't be working tomorrow, or Christmas Day." Before he could stop her, she hugged him then stepped back. "Take care of yourself, Marty."

"Merry Christmas." Gruffly, Marty gave her a searching look.

Rushing away, Megan went back to her car and drove to the town's park. She buttoned her coat and she headed toward a picnic table. Using a gloved hand, she brushed the snow off the top then climbed to sit on it, staring out at the park.

A couple of minutes later, she heard a vehicle behind her, and then the sound of a door opening and closing.

"Hey, why'd you want to meet me here?" Cole asked, moving around the table. His beautiful face was excited. He must think she had a special Christmas present for him. The happiness in his face died when he noticed the serious expression on her face.

Cole reached out to take her hands in his. "What's wrong?"

"Nothing," she lied. "I've come to a decision."

Cole's eyes met hers. "Somehow, I don't think I'm going to like whatever decision you made. What is it?"

"I've decided to leave Treepoint—tomorrow."

"Where are you going?"

"I haven't decided yet. When I do, I'll text you my address."

"I have one better." Cole's jaw clenched stubbornly. "We can leave together. I already decided to change my plans to stay here until the New Year. We can go on a road trip together instead."

"No, Cole. It's better if I go alone. You can come visit me after I get settled."

"I don't understand. Why did you ask if it was okay for you to fall in love with me if you were just going to take off out of the blue?"

"I thought it over. We're moving too fast. We need time apart to reevaluate whether we're right for each other." The whole time she held Cole's gaze, she couldn't bear the hurt on his face.

"I love you—"

"You don't know me well enough to love me. I'll never fit in your life. We move in different circles. You're friends with celebrities, you run your own business—"

"You do, too," he insisted.

Her lips quirked in a smile. "There's no comparison."

"Maybe not now ... but you're just starting out. If you don't want to deliver anymore, we'll find something else for you. I don't care if you work, anyway. I can take care of you. I want to—"

Megan shook her hands free, jumped off the picnic table, and hugged him tightly, going onto her toes to kiss his cheek. "Cole, it's better for me to leave ... before one of us gets hurt."

"Too late ... Please, don't leave me," he begged. "Don't take off like this. Let's go back to the hotel and talk."

Megan couldn't hold back her tears. Not wanting him to see, she dropped her arms from around him. "I don't trust myself in a hotel with you. That's why I wanted to meet you here." Unable to control her bottom lip trembling, she bit down on it. "I'm weak where you're concerned."

Turning to face the empty playground, she moved to stand by his side. "Look at how beautiful the snow is. You need a woman like that to love ... not someone like me. Your stepfather nearly destroyed you; I'll be damned if I finish the job for him. I'd rather leave you brokenhearted for now, so you can find a woman who deserves you."

She guessed she did have another piece of her heart to lose.

Megan started to move away from his side, but Cole caught her by the arm. His expression tore at her heart.

"Here I thought you brought me here to give me my Christmas present," he said hoarsely.

"Me leaving is my gift to you."

Twenty-Two

Tired, Megan brushed her curly hair then checked the mirror before gathering the clothes she had slept in last night. Shoving the sweater and jeans into a plastic bag, she looked down at herself. The simple black dress she had bought off the clearance rack in town was shorter than she would have liked, but once she put on her black coat, she felt better about her appearance.

A knock on the door had her taking a final glance before unlocking it.

"Sorry ..."

The teenager didn't appear interested in any excuse she wanted to make. She just wanted her out to use the restroom.

Megan moved toward the beverage station to pour herself a large coffee and chose a cheese Danish to eat on the way to the Coleman's.

"You look pretty today," Joel complimented her when she went to pay. "You heading to the church?"

"You could say that. Any problems getting the car transferred over?"

"No, I made it just in time before the office closed. I don't know what the rush was that I needed to get it done on my lunch hour, but I got it done."

"It saves me money on my insurance," she lied. Megan didn't want any loose ends when she left town. "How much do I owe you?"

"Nothing. The coffee and the Danish are on me. Merry Christmas."

"Thank you. Merry Christmas."

She walked to her car parked at the pumps and got in. The car was fueled and ready to go once her daughter's funeral was over.

Eating the Danish without tasting it, she drove to the Coleman's property. The pastor was already there, talking to Silas.

She got out of the car and went to the back seat to open a small box. Taking the teddy bear, she clasped it in her hand as she closed the door.

As she walked to where the two men were standing by the porch, she managed a smile. "Good morning."

"Good morning," both men returned her greeting.

"Are you ready to begin the service?" the pastor asked.

"Yes, whenever you are." She nodded at the pastor then turned to Silas. "We won't be long. I don't want to hold you up from where you're going."

Silas frowned, looking confused. "I wasn't leaving. I'm going to your daughter's funeral, if that's all right?"

Megan pressed her lips together, trying not to cry. "That would be more than all right." She gave him a watery smile.

"Good." Silas encouragingly patted her shoulder. "I won't be a minute." Moving away from her, he went up the steps to his porch to open the door.

Thinking he was going inside to grab a thicker coat, she was shocked when, one after another, the Colemans stepped outside, dressed in dark suits, like Silas was. Even Ginny and her husband came out, making her hold the teddy bear closer to her at their kindness. When the last person walked out, she nearly lost the control she had managed to hold on to so far.

Cole approached her with a somber expression, holding out his arm for her to take.

Blinking back tears, Megan curled her arm through his as the pastor led the way to the small cemetery.

As the cemetery came into sight, the tears she had fought so hard to hold back began to fall. Townspeople were lined up, making a path for them to walk through. Then, as they passed, they fell in, creating a progression to the small hole that had a white casket waiting to be lowered into the ground.

Taking the handkerchief Cole handed her, she moved to the casket to place the teddy bear on top.

"Let's begin."

As the pastor spoke, Megan imagined what might have been, what her daughter would have looked like, imagined her as a toddler, at two, five, eight, even imagined how excited she would have been to receive her first kiss, graduated high school, college, trying on her wedding dress, her wedding day ... all the same dreams she'd had for her when she was pregnant. That she had never seen those beautiful dreams come true was a sorrow she would carry for the rest of her life.

"God, Megan is entrusting Maliah into Your care, to share in the enteral light of Your presence until they will be reunited again. You may have been denied holding Maliah on earth, Megan, but in Heaven, you will hold her for eternity."

Sobbing, she turned toward Cole to be held tightly in his arms. Then Megan forced herself to watch as Silas, Isaac, and Jacob lowered the casket into the ground. Only when it was completely covered with dirt did Cole turn her away from the grave and Megan realized the crowd had left.

"They left after the service. They're waiting at the house."

Megan felt inadequate at what to say to Cole after hurting

him the day before, and yet he still showed up to help her through an ordeal that she didn't know if she could have made it through without him.

"How did you find out I was having a service for Maliah?"

"You're not the only one who can't keep a secret."

"I can't believe so many people came." Tearful, Megan twisted the handkerchief in her hands. "I saw Winter and Viper."

When they crossed the knob of the hill, Megan frowned. Since she had parked her car, two white tents had been raised. Underneath were tables and chairs. Another tent had been set off to the side, where people were placing food on three tables.

"They're holding a funeral reception for me?"

Cole turned her to face him. "It's not a funeral reception." He tenderly cupped her cheek. "They're giving you a homecoming."

Twenty-Three

L aying her head on Cole's chest, she took a deep, sobbing breath. So many people were there. She had thought she would be burying Maliah alone with only the pastor, yet here, Willa was organizing the food trays and desserts, which Megan had been sure were meant for the church dinner. The Last Riders were taking outdoor heaters out of trucks and placing them in the tents so everyone could be warm. The Colemans were carrying chairs from a van, placing them around the tables.

Raising the handkerchief, she wiped her damp cheeks when she saw Greer slowly walking toward a table, his hair snow white. Watching him, she couldn't help but laugh when she saw him poke Dustin with his cane when he was about to take the chair Greer clearly wanted.

"Let's get you something to eat."

Megan raised her head to look at Cole then at all the people who had come. Her jaw set in a firm line. They had come for her today ... and when they had tried to help her, she had refused to give them what they needed. All because of fear. The same reason why she had planned to leave after the service. She had spent the majority of her life in fear ... and she was done.

She took a step back from Cole and looked him straight in the eyes. "I love you with all of my heart," she confessed. "I never realized I could love someone this much, but I do."

"I love you." He grinned. "You're not leaving?"

"I'm going to leave that up to you"—Megan nodded at the crowd of people—"and them."

Cole frowned. "What does that mean?"

Megan moved away without answering. Walking to the tables, she raised her hands in the air. "Would everyone please have a seat? I would like to say something before you eat."

Megan waited until all the chairs were filled or people had moved to where they could see her.

"I want to thank everyone for coming to Maliah's service and going to so much trouble for me. I don't deserve your kindness. I didn't deserve it when you tried to save me from Curt and I threw your help back in your face." Megan pinpointed one face in the crowd, nodding in her direction. "I let Jo stand alone to fight against someone evil, holding my silence at her expense. I'm sorry, Jo. I'm truly sorry."

Megan tore her gaze away from Jo's. Shaking, she returned her focus back to the crowd. As she did, she felt Cole move closer to stand behind her, wrapping an arm around her waist.

"I wish I had a better excuse, other than I was a coward. I still am, actually. You see, after Maliah's funeral, I was going to run away because I was too afraid something would come out that I didn't want anyone in town to know. My pride was more important than stopping Curt." Megan gave them a bittersweet smile. "Karma is a bitch. I didn't want to be humiliated or shamed if I told anyone Curt had touched me when he worked at the school. Then, here comes Karma, showing me that I shamed and humiliated myself when I couldn't accept the loss of my baby."

Winter rose from her chair. "Megan, you don't need to do this."

"I do, Mrs. James. I want you and everyone else to understand why I acted the way I did—"

"We found out not long after Curt's death," Winter revealed.

"About the pictures?"

Megan felt like a little girl when Winter took her hands into hers, unaware droplets of tears were falling to her cheeks.

"Yes."

Shamed to her soul, Magen started to sob. "You saw—"

Megan felt herself pulled into Winter's arms. Sobbing, she leaned into Winter like she had wished she could have her mother, crying tears she had needed to shed years ago from a pain that had scorched her soul from having her trust betrayed. Winter gave her what she had been denied when she needed it the most—a mother's loving touch.

When she was able to stop crying, Winter took her handkerchief away to wipe her cheeks. "I don't want you worrying about those pictures anymore," Mrs. James said in her no-nonsense voice. "Viper's brother will make sure none of them will ever appear on the Internet, nor any other of Curt's other victims."

Megan searched Winter's eyes. She wouldn't give her Chelsea's name, but at the same time, she also wanted to make sure she wouldn't have to live with her own fear any longer. "What if any of them are afraid their pictures will be found? Someone had my pictures I didn't know about. Curt gave them to—"

"We know what Curt did." Winter nodded her head to the side.

Megan turned her head to find Chelsea with a man whom Megan assumed was her boyfriend.

"Cole went to the hotel and had a talk with Chelsea.

Harford had called and told him what he overheard when you and Chelsea were talking in your room. Chelsea gave all of your pictures and the phone Curt kept them on to Cole. He destroyed everything. Cole was also able to reassure Chelsea that hers had already been taken care of. Everyone has a clean slate."

"I was going to leave," Megan admitted.

Winter looked over her shoulder. "You might have told yourself that, but you wouldn't have."

"I don't know about that." Megan shook her head. Winter had more faith her than she had in herself.

Winter tilted her head. "Then why did you ask Lucky to perform the service for Maliah? You knew he would tell us. Just like you knew the Colemans would tell Cole. You wouldn't have if you hadn't wanted us to stop you. Sadly, I don't think you will be with us for long. Cole's planning to steal you away from us again," she laughingly warned.

Megan turned to look over her shoulder at Cole. "He is?"

Cole turned her to him. "I am, but we can come back every Christmas," he promised, pulling her into his arms.

So happy she wanted to scream with joy, she had to constrain herself. She had just buried her daughter, and it was a solemn occasion. She shouldn't be this happy ...

Unable to help herself, Megan looked skyward.

"What are you looking at?" Cole asked, nuzzling her neck.

"Have you ever been in a hot air balloon?"

He raised his head to look upward, searching the sky. "No. Have you?"

Megan gave him a tender smile. "Oh yes ... it's miraculous."

Epilogue

～～～

After leaving the Christmas service at the church, Cole drove her to the Last Riders' clubhouse for Christmas dinner. She had accepted the invitation from Viper the day before, and regardless of his kindness, she was still wary of him.

"Why are you so nervous?" Cole asked, placing a supportive arm around her waist as he returned from helping Rider carry food inside.

"I'm not nervous."

Cole raised a quizzical brow and took the plastic cup she was holding away from her. "Then why have you been glued to the same spot for the last ten minutes?"

"Is your sister here yet?" Megan asked, unintentionally revealing the cause of her worry.

"No. Casey and Lily are still dealing with an emergency at Shade's house."

Concerned, Megan forgot her nervousness. "What emergency?"

"Max raided the refrigerator last night and ate most of the dessert meant for dinner today."

"Oh no." Megan giggled. "I bet the women are furious with him."

Cole grinned. "Max is denying it. He's pinning the blame on the kids."

"Then how do they know Max is the one responsible?"

Cole gave her a wide grin.

"You didn't."

"I did. He ate the pie Casey made for me."

When the line was formed for making plates, Cole turned to her.

"I'm going to go check on Casey and Lily. They may need an extra pair of hands."

"Okay."

Megan watched Cole walk out a door in the kitchen. Scanning the long line, Megan curiously went out the door as well. There were several tables outside with a barbeque pit which had been covered for the winter. Enjoying the cool air after the heated kitchen, Megan decided to wait at one of the tables until Cole returned.

Swiping off the snow with a gloved hand, she was able to watch through the windows and back door as the Last Riders happily made their plates. *I almost missed this*, she thought achingly. Emotions were overwhelming her. This Christmas was vastly different than how she had expected it to be when she crossed that bridge a few short weeks ago.

Laughter filling her ears made her turn to see children running around the corner behind a house ahead. They were picking up handfuls of snow, forming them into snowballs before launching them at each other. Megan only let herself smile at the cute scene for a moment, knowing her daughter would have been right there with them if she were still on this earth.

Looking back through the windows, she was about to

head inside when she realized the line for the food had dissipated some, but a small voice from behind her caused her to freeze in place.

"Hi!"

Megan looked back to find a little girl bundled up from head to toe in a lavender snowsuit that resembled Ralphie's brother from the *Christmas Story*. Like the mom from the movie, her mother must've gone overboard bundling her up. She wanted to laugh, but the small, pink-cheeked face and nose instinctively told her who she was before she gave her name.

"I'm Aisha!"

She was afraid she might frighten the little girl, so it took her a few moments to blink back tears before she could keep her voice from cracking. "I'm Megan." Quickly, she wiped her eye that couldn't hold in all the water before it spilled onto her cheek. She finally got herself under control, unable to keep from laughing at the cuteness overload. At first, she thought only a mother could dress their child like that, but now she knew the real culprit. "You look so cute in your purple snowsuit. Let me guess ... your daddy dressed you today?"

"Mmhmm!" Aisha waddled closer to her, trying her best to get up on the bench beside her. "And now I can't play."

It was like watching a baby penguin fight for its life to get on the bench as Aisha still had yet to manage to do so.

Tears now escaped her eyes, but it wasn't out of sadness; it was out of sheer joy from laughing so hard. She only hesitated a moment before picking the little girl up. The last time she had done so, Aisha was a newborn. Now, five years later, Megan's life was completely different. She'd been so fearful of how she would react around children, Aisha was like fresh air blowing the fear away.

"Will you pleaseee take it off for me so I can play and

throw a snowball back at John?" Aisha cried. "I promise not to tell Daddy."

Megan might be a different person who held the trust of the town again and, most importantly, Viper's. But she wasn't stupid.

"How about we build a snowman instead?"